P9-CJC-798

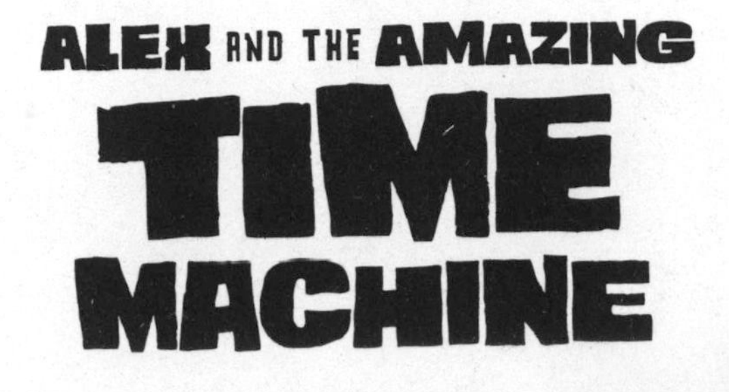
ALEX AND THE AMAZING
TIME
MACHINE

# ALEX AND THE AMAZING TIME MACHINE

RICH COHEN

WITH ILLUSTRATIONS BY KELLY MURPHY



Christy Ottaviano Books
Henry Holt and Company • New York

Henry Holt and Company, LLC
*Publishers since 1866*
175 Fifth Avenue
New York, New York 10010
mackids.com



Library of Congress Cataloging-in-Publication Data
Cohen, Rich.
Alex and the amazing time machine / Rich Cohen ; [illustrated by
Kelly Murphy]. — 1st ed.
p. cm.
"Christy Ottaviano Books."
Summary: Fifth-grader Alex Trumble builds a "dingus"—a time machine—
when his brother Steven is kidnapped by dangerous, evil time-travelers,
to get back to the past and into the future to save his family from disaster.
ISBN 978-0-8050-9418-3 (hc)
[1. Inventions—Fiction. 2. Time travel—Fiction. 3. Adventure and
adventurers—Fiction. 4. Science fiction.] I. Murphy, Kelly, ill. II. Title.
PZ7.C6633A1 2012 [Fic]—dc23 2011033476

First Edition—2012 / Designed by April Ward
Printed in the United States of America by R. R. Donnelley & Sons
Company, Harrisonburg, Virginia

1 3 5 7 9 10 8 6 4 2

*For Aaron, Nate, Micah*

*And, of course, Todd Johnston—*
*I salute you, my brother.*

# CONTENTS

# A NOTE TO READERS

One day, when I was ten and just back home after a long day at the beach, my best friend, Todd Johnston, and I fell upon the freezer like Vikings. We planned to devour and be happy with the devastation we caused. But when I looked in the freezer, and this, like many things in my life, was the fault of my mother, there was but one Dreamsicle. The rest of the bounty—pops and drumsticks, pints of ice cream—was gone, all gone.

"Who gets it?" asked Todd, fixing me with a cool blue glare.

"There's also a banana," I told him. "One of us can have that, and you know, it's good for you."

"Who gets it?" Todd repeated.

I proposed a best-of-three series: Rock, Paper, Scissors.

Todd agreed.

The games commenced.

Though I normally fare well in such contests, this time, with the treat in the balance, I went down in a sweep.

Todd took the Dreamsicle. I took the banana, humbled by my loss. But when I pulled back the peel, an amazing thing revealed itself: not one banana but two, side by side—a freak, an oddity, a miracle.

"My God," I said, "twins!"

Todd cried foul. He'd won, but now, suddenly, his victory did not seem so clear. It was a key moment for me, and I've remembered the lesson ever since: no matter how it looks, you just can't tell the losers from the winners while the ball is still in play.

—Rich Cohen

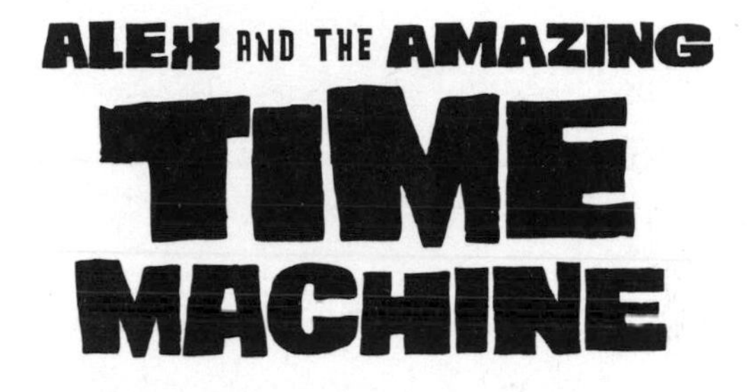
ALEX AND THE AMAZING
TIME
MACHINE

# 1

# THE BOY WHO LIVED IN TIME

When people ask Alex Trumble where he lives, he is always careful to tell them not just the number of the house and the name of the street and town, but also the date and the year: 1062 Bluff Road, Glencoe, Illinois, March 29, 2012.

"If you want to find me," he explains, "you need to know where I am, but also when I am."

The kids in Alex Trumble's school thought he was a little funny. Not *ha-ha* funny—though he was—but just sort of different. He spent a lot of time reading books, very old books filled with drawings and words few people could understand. He spoke of hidden dimensions and time warps. He did most of this talking with just one kid, his best friend, Todd Johnston.

Here's the funny part. With a kid like Alex, who is happy in a library, you expect his best friend to be another kid like Alex. There were not a lot of those, of course, but a few kids came close. Tommy Ryan, for example, who sat in the front row in math class with his hand raised. Or Debbie Bernstein, whose hair coiled like red springs. A founding member of the model rocket club, Debbie was famous for the voyage of *Big Bertha*, which carried six eggs into the stratosphere behind North School before parachuting into the sandbox next to the jungle gym.

Todd Johnston was nothing like that. He was big and sunny and always outside. In the summer, his hair got so blond it was white, and his knuckles were tanned and cracked. He was the best athlete at North, but not the sort of best athlete who is arrogant about it. He didn't think because he hit the softball over the fence fifteen times that year that he was better than anyone else. Maybe that's why he was such great friends with Alex. They were different, but they were also a lot alike—each in his own way was special, and each in his own way thought there was nothing very special about it. In fact, Alex was constantly troubled by fears of his own ordinariness. "When will I distinguish myself?" he asked Todd.

"When you stop trying," his friend told him.

They were in fifth grade, which they agreed was the best grade so far. In kindergarten, they treat you like a baby, and you are a baby. In second grade, they treat you like a baby, but you're not a baby. You're something else. No one knows what for sure, but you are not a baby. You can cut and paste and glue, but you can also charm and trick and fool. Not a baby. In fifth grade, the assignments take shape, and the teacher talks in a clear, straightforward way.

Alex and Todd walked home together from school unless Todd had a practice or a game, which, to be honest, was a lot of the time. If Todd did have a practice or a game, Alex would sit in the bleachers taking notes. He often had ideas for plays or suggestions for ways Todd could improve his swing. Todd listened to these ideas, nodding. He knew Alex well enough to know that was just the kind of kid he was. Full of ideas, schemes, plots, and plans. He wanted to help.

On most days, they followed Vernon Road into

town, which consisted of a dozen streets on a hill above Lake Michigan.

Like a lot of average-seeming American towns, there was something strange about Glencoe. An odd, otherworldly energy crackled beneath the surface. And that's not even taking into consideration all the people on the outskirts who believed they'd been abducted by aliens. Every now and then, a kid would go to sleep in his bed in Glencoe and wake up in a house halfway across Cook County. Whenever this happened, people just figured the aliens had goofed, beamed someone up for examination, then accidentally returned them to the wrong house. It was not the kidnapping that bothered the locals so much as this sloppy inattention to detail.

When Alex and Todd got beyond the last sidewalk, they hopped a fence and cut across backyards, a private world of ponds and gardens that could be followed, without touching cement, all the way to the beach. If Alex was with any other kid, his mother wouldn't let him walk home without an adult. But Alex was not with any other kid. Mrs. Trumble knew Todd would look out for her son and make sure he got home safely, no matter the obstacle.

The Trumbles' house, depending on your point of view, was either a wreck or wonderful. It had been a fancy mansion once, owned by a powerful businessman, a tycoon, but the tycoon had been involved in a scandal. He lost his money, and the house fell apart. It was a glorious ruin, a maze of sitting rooms, sunrooms, libraries, parlors, and secret passages. From the top floors, you could see Lake Michigan crashing onto the rocks below.

The Trumbles were not wealthy. Mr. Trumble was a writer of books that few people read, but he wasn't sad about it. "Time is funny," he would say. "I could be writing the right stories, just writing them at the wrong time."

When Alex asked about this, Mr. Trumble would shrug and say, "Maybe I have a huge audience, and a lot of people love my books—they just don't know it yet."

"When will they know it?" asked Alex.

"Later," said Mr. Trumble. "A lot of things that don't make sense now will be clear later."

The house was like that, too. It was a mess in the present, but Alex's father was able to see what it would look like in the future, after it had been restored.

Mr. and Mrs. Trumble had bought the house for next to nothing. It was owned by the bank and had been empty for years. When Alex talked about the sad history of the house, his mother told him to forget about it. If he asked why, she said, "Because you can't do anything about the past."

Mrs. Trumble had short brown hair and big green eyes. She was a lawyer and worked in the city. She defended innocent people wrongly accused of terrible crimes. She often worked for free, because it was the right thing to do. Alex was proud to have a mother like that.

Todd and Alex came in the back door, threw down their bags, then went into the living room, where Steven Trumble, Alex's brother, was watching baseball on TV. Steven looked like Alex, only older, bigger. If you made a Silly Putty copy of Alex and stretched it, you would have Steven. He was mean, too, and cynical. He said things like "It takes a sucker." Or "If you are fooled, you are a fool."

Steven questioned Alex about the baseball season ahead.

"How do the Cubs look?"

"What do you think of the division?"

"How does the pitching stack up?"

All the Trumbles knew Alex was a genius, and they used his gift to their own ends. Alex's father used it to help him pick stocks in the newspaper. Nothing was certain, said Alex, but much could be guessed, so he guessed on stocks, and mostly he guessed right. Mr. Trumble felt guilty using his son this way, but he needed the money. Alex's brother used Alex's genius to figure out the winners of baseball and basketball games. That's how, each spring, Steven Trumble won the NCAA pool at school.

Even so, Steven found his brother annoying. Some of this was classic big-brother-little-brother stuff. The fact was, Steven had a vague memory of the world before Alex, when he had it all—the toys, the parents, everything—to himself. As far as Steven was concerned, Alex was now using up air, time, and love that really belonged to him.

Of course, none of this was said out loud. Maybe Steven didn't even know about it, not in a front-of-the-mind way. Instead, it was sublimated, which is a nice way of saying it was stepped on and covered up and squashed down until it popped out in all sorts of unexpected ways—the charley horse, the shoulder squeeze, the nasty remark: "I know you are, but what am I?" "That's so funny I forgot to laugh." "Shut up, doofus!"

What's more, Steven and Alex, though in some

ways a lot alike, had different interests. Steven, for example, was obsessed with sports. It was what he cared about more than anything. Alex loved sports, too, but he was also into books, ideas, made-up things, and schemes. He was a dreamer. Steven did not get this side of his brother at all. He often heard people call Alex clever, but he never understood what this cleverness amounted to: did it ever save a life, win a game, impress a girl? Whenever Alex walked into Steven's room to tell him about some new invention or idea—Alex never stopped trying—Steven would roll his eyes and say, "You should stick with baseball."

Worst of all was the way Alex seemed to feel about Steven's occasional scorn. He didn't care. When they were younger, in the heat of an argument, Steven once shouted, "I hate you, Alex." And the way Alex responded, well, it captured everything that drove Steven crazy: "That's okay—I love you enough for both of us."

The best part of the house was the turret, which was like a tower in a castle. It was fifty feet high, a needle of brick with windows scattered along a spiral staircase that went up and up. There was a big, round, glassed-in room at the top from where you could see the lake clear to the horizon.

When the Trumbles moved into the house, an inspector from the town examined the turret. He took measurements and made notations before calling the structure "unsound" and putting a board over the entrance on the first floor. This did not stop Todd and Alex. Late one night, when the wind was blowing, they loosened the board with the claw end of a hammer and climbed the tower. It was shadowy and strange at the top. The windows rattled; the floorboards creaked; the room swayed like the deck of a ship.

The tower became their clubhouse. Alex had books up there, flashlights, sleeping bags, and a radio. The walls were covered with posters, pictures, and articles Alex had cut out of newspapers and magazines. If you were a detective, you'd be able to get a good sense of Alex just by studying the walls of this room.

There were stills from his favorite movies, *Twelve Monkeys* and *Time Bandits*. There were copies of his favorite books, *The Outsiders* and *The Strange Life of Ivan Osokin*. There were photographs of his favorite baseball players, but since most of them did not play for the Cubs, he had cut Cub uniforms out of the paper and taped them over the pictures. Stephen Strasburg, Joe Mauer, Robinson Cano—in Alex Trumble's mind, they were all Cubs. There were pictures of animals, too. Not satisfied with the animals that existed, Alex cut and pasted the pictures into hybrids. There was an eagle with the body of a bear, a dingo with the claws of a lion, a giraffe with the head of a Tasmanian devil. Laughing at these, Todd said, "Dude, you're turning into a mad scientist!"

Todd and Alex spent hours in the turret, talking about baseball, school, nothing at all, but, sooner or later, Alex always gave in to his obsession, the nature of time. "It's a real thing," he told Todd, lying back, staring at the ceiling, "just like the sidewalk from here to town is a real thing."

"Then where is it?" Todd asked.

"It's all around."

"So why can't I see it?"

"Why doesn't a fish see the water?" Alex said, sitting up. "Because he's in it. Hours, minutes, days. You're in them like a fish is in the water. It's where you live, and you don't even know it."

That night, Alex had a strange dream. Well, he had many strange dreams. In one, he was wearing a cape and flying low and fast over a city. In another, he was falling from a tower, falling and falling in a way that made it seem like he would never stop. But in the dream I'm thinking of, he was on solid ground in his best clothes, a jet-setter, traveling not from country to country but from age to age, from present to past.

He was a time traveler, sailing via a device of his own creation. It was made of a laser pointer and an iPod, and it opened a warp in space through which Alex could skip across time. He saw time tunnels and planets and good people and bad, his parents, of course, his dog, his best friend, his brother—something terrible was happening to his brother—but there were other people, too. He kept seeing two faces in particular, but they were never clear enough to identify. These were men from the future, he could feel it, themselves part of a cosmic plot, a conspiracy Alex had gotten tangled in as you get tangled in the sheets just before dawn, when you can no longer tell the difference between what has happened, what will happen, and what you've only dreamed.

# 2

# CARL AND LITTLE DAVY

Alex went to the public library early the next morning. The building was on Park Avenue, the main street in town. Alex took the front steps two at a time, then pushed open the front doors. He would normally nod to the librarian and head to the science reading room in back, where he sat by himself, paging through ancient encyclopedias. Sometimes people learned something, something important, which was later forgotten. It had been discovered and written down, then lost. Some of these things, secrets that had not always been secret, can still be found in the oldest books. That's what Alex believed, and that's what he searched for in the reading room. But this morning, before he could even get his bag off his shoulder, the librarian pulled him into a closet off the entryway.

She was a nice woman with gray hair and so old it was hard to calculate her exact age. Her name was Ms. Reagan. One thing about her was unusual for a librarian. She was incredibly loud. Maybe it had to do with her hearing aid or her wish to be understood, but she was one of the loudest people Alex had ever met. This always made him uneasy, but it made him especially uneasy now, as she was telling him about a strange thing that had just happened.

"Two men were in here asking about you," Ms. Reagan yelled. "They did not seem like nice men. In fact, I was thinking of calling the police. Or your parents."

"Who were they?" asked Alex, his heart pounding.

"There was a tall one," Ms. Reagan said. "He was skinny. And a short one. He was fat. The tall one spoke a lot, and the short one spoke even more."

"But who were they?"

"I don't know who they were, but they know who you are."

"What do they know about me?"

"They know you live in that big house near the

lake, they know your name, they know what you read. Yes," she added, as if speaking to herself, "I should call your parents."

"What do you mean, they know what I read?"

"They know you read in the science room, that you've been looking at old books about space and time."

"How do they know that?"

"I don't know," said Ms. Reagan, "but they wanted a list of all the books you've checked out in the last year."

"Did you give it to them?"

"Oh, dear, no. Being a librarian is like being a doctor or a policeman. It's a trust. What you read is your business. What do you think they want?"

"I don't know," said Alex, thinking. "Maybe I stumbled across something in one of those books, something I wasn't supposed to see."

"Well, they did go back and poke around the science room," said Ms. Reagan.

"Are they still there?" asked Alex, fear in his voice.

"No. They left about fifteen minutes ago."

Alex thanked Ms. Reagan and told her he was going back to the reading room himself. "Maybe I can figure out what they were looking for," he explained.

"Be careful," said Ms. Reagan. "Those were bad men."

"Bad how?"

"When I said you had not been in and were not coming in, the short, fat, slow one grabbed my wrist and gave it a hard squeeze. There was a lot of anger in that squeeze."

Before Alex left, he turned and said, "Please don't call my parents. I'll tell my dad when I get home. I'm sure there's a simple explanation."

"I think I really must tell someone, perhaps Sheriff Bonneville," said Ms. Reagan.

"No," said Alex. "Don't do that. I just remembered: it's all a game."

"A game?"

"Yes, part of a scavenger hunt for the Boy Scouts. We're supposed to find the clues without getting tagged by the bad guys. That's who you saw: parents who volunteered to be bad guys."

"Really?" said Ms. Reagan. "Well, that is a hoot. But I wish they would tell us of these things in advance. It gave me a scare."

"If they told you," said Alex, "it wouldn't seem half as real."

"I suppose that's so," said Ms. Reagan.

Alex was pleased with his ability to come up with this off the top of his head. It would keep him in control of the adventure that was beginning to unfold. He was nervous about the bad men, but excited, too. It seemed like a chance to finally distinguish himself.

Once Ms. Reagan had calmed down, Alex went back to the science reading room, which was a mess. Books had been pulled off the shelves and scattered across the floor. As soon as Alex got over his initial shock, he began digging through the piles, searching for a rare and precious text called *Light Beams and Indians.*

How did Alex first come across this book?

Well, that's a story.

Over the previous few months, Alex had become obsessed with a scientist named Shari Ali Ben Shaprut. To be fair, he was obsessed less with Dr. Shaprut than with a book she had written to make sense of her own terrible life. It was called *Cosmic Redo: How to Build a Machine So We Can Go Back and Fix All the Things That Went Wrong, Wrong, Wrong.* There was a lot of math and science in the book, but what interested Alex most was the motivation behind the doctor's quest to break the time barrier.

When the doctor was still too young to reason,

her family went to see a circus in a field outside of Shreveport, Louisiana. Someone had forgotten to secure the latch on the elephant pen. The blast of the human cannonball sent the elephants running, and the doctor's entire family—save the doctor herself, who was safe in the concession tent—was crushed in the stampede. For years, decades even, the doctor had been trying to build a time machine so she could return to the past and secure the latch on the elephant pen. A sad and beautiful quest, thought Alex.

Alex found Dr. Shaprut's e-mail address online. She was a teacher at one of those ivy-covered schools in the East. She was a strange woman, driven by a single desire, who, in the course of all her searching, had run into an obstacle, a problem that could not be fixed. She was like a speedster with a blown tire and was stuck on the side of the road, waiting for help that might never arrive. As a result, she welcomed Alex's interest. They were soon e-mailing, spitballing, problem solving. It was several weeks before Dr. Shaprut realized that readytotrumble@aol.com was neither a retired professor nor a half-crazed time travel aficionado, but a kid from a town near Chicago. By then, the doctor was so deep in the nitty-gritty with Alex, she didn't care.

It was Dr. Shaprut who pointed Alex to the esoteric text *Light Beams and Indians.* In case you're wondering, *esoteric*, used by me, here, means a strange, out-of-print, nearly impossible to find notebook that was almost lost when the world switched from books in libraries and bookstores to text on screens. It was written by an explorer of the western grasslands named Cornelius Conner Cruise O'Connell, but whom everyone, even his closest friends, knew as the Buckskinned Philosopher. He appeared in the middle of the 1800s, wrote articles and books for ten years, then vanished mysteriously. During this time, he wandered the wilds, grappled with grizzly bears and moose, forded streams, and stared at the northern lights. A single likeness of him survives, less a portrait than a sketch. It shows a fair-skinned, narrow-eyed man dressed in fur, smiling in the way of a person who knows something big that you do not know.

The copies of the book were reproductions of a handwritten diary. The margins were filled with notes in the same hand. In other words, the philosopher composed the book, then added thoughts and ideas as the years went by. It was filled with descriptions and poems, snatches of overheard dialogue and tidbits. Now and then, the philosopher included, in his clearly identifiable handwriting, numbers and equations, insights he had in the dead of night when, sitting on some mountain peak, he experienced the universe as a single organism, a wild, living thing.

Though all of this was interesting, Alex didn't understand what it had to do with time travel.

"Well, the fact is," wrote Dr. Shaprut, "this man, who lived before cars and planes, spoke in a way that suggests he achieved a breakthrough that will one day make time travel possible. He learned a secret, and it's hidden in that book."

"Where in the book?" asked Alex.

"Not sure," the doctor wrote back. "It might be in a common phrase or sentence, anywhere really."

When Alex asked Dr. Shaprut why she hadn't found the secret herself, she said, "Even if the truth is right in front of me, I might miss it. The fact is, I might not be as well equipped as you to spot the key detail."

"How's that possible?" wrote Alex.

"I know more stuff than you do," Dr. Shaprut replied, "because I'm older and I've been searching a long time, but this might be my weakness. You have new eyes, fresh eyes, and are less likely to pass over and miss the pattern hidden in the rug."

Alex began searching for *Light Beams and Indians.* There had been hundreds of copies once, but, over the years, most of them had vanished. This was itself a riddle no librarian could explain. But Alex happened to live in the very spot where the Buckskinned Philosopher had written the diary, which was an advantage. Copies had been scattered across the Midwest. Alex searched every library and storage facility in the area.

Late one afternoon, as the sun was setting over the very same grasslands, now filled with housing developments and malls, he found the book in the basement of the Near North Historical Society in Wheaton, amid the collections of ancient canoes, arrowheads, and maps. It was sort of miraculous, or else the kind of good fortune you must teach yourself not to question. The society was affiliated with the Illinois public libraries, and that's how Alex had the book transferred to Glencoe. Alex had gone through the pages carefully. Though it was never less than cool, he did not find any secrets.

That's the background on the book Alex was anxiously searching for in the science room of the

Glencoe Public Library, which, as I said, was a mess. It took twenty minutes of digging and searching the debris, but he finally found the journal under a pile of old books, tossed aside by the bad men as if it was garbage.

Alex lifted it onto a reading table and opened it up to the middle. At first, he did not believe his eyes. The pages he had been reading on his last visit were gone, ripped clean from the binding. Something about this tear, the nature of the rip, made Alex nervous. There was violence in it, the result being a jagged scar down the spine of the book. Looking at this tear, Alex could see the fingers of the fat man closed around Ms. Reagan's wrist, then, in a flash, he could see the same fingers closed around his own neck.

He examined the book, noting what pages had been torn out: 567 to 601. The secret must be hidden in those pages, he told himself, writing the numbers on a piece of paper. He pulled his backpack over his shoulders and hurried into the streets of town.

When you feel like you're being watched, everything looks suspicious. The clerks in the bank looked like secret agents. The girl in the pet store looked like a spy. The man in the flower shop looked like a killer.

Town Hall was creepy. St. Stephen's Church was odd. The pharmacy was just plain weird.

As Alex turned onto a side street, he spotted his reflection in the window of the real estate office. For a moment, he didn't recognize himself. Who is that kid, he wondered, and why's he staring at me?

Have I told you what Alex looks like? Dashingly handsome, that's what, with wavy brown hair and light green eyes. He had been growing a lot over the last year, and as a result, his pants were too short for his legs and his sleeves were too short for his arms and his coat was snug around his chest.

If teased about this, he would say, "I've got bigger fish to fry."

When he realized he had been scared by his own reflection, he felt ashamed. He valued bravery but worried, in his heart, that maybe he was not so brave after all.

He took a left and headed down the alley behind the candy store. Doing this, he figured, would keep him away from any dangerous characters, but, as soon as he made the turn, a white van zoomed up, cutting off the road ahead. When he turned back, he saw a big man walking toward him from behind. His hands

were like bear paws and hung in front of him. His mouth was a sneer. And he was fat, not that jiggly, soft, jolly kind of fat but the hard, mean, cannonball kind of fat. Looking at a guy like that, you could imagine three or four different ways he might kill you: with his hands around your neck, with his body crushing you into a fence, with his feet stomping on your windpipe.

Alex stood frozen. It's funny, he thought, I came into this alley to get away from this guy, but by coming into this alley, I ran into him instead. By trying to avoid it, I made it happen. As Alex was thinking this, three moments went by. In moment one, he was watching the fat man as the fat man walked toward him. In moment two, he was still watching the fat man. In moment three, the fat man had his fat fingers around Alex's neck and had begun to squeeze.

Just then, two honks came from the van. The fat man looked over. A thin-faced man was behind the steering wheel. Have you ever seen the belly of a snake? Well, his skin looked just like that. There should, in fact, be a color called snake-belly white. You should be able to go into a paint store and buy a quart and pick up swatches, though I can't imagine anyone wanting to use it in a nursery or a living room. It's a unique sort of white, dirty with a green wash, and it always looks oily, even on a bone-dry day. And his eyes—they were so pale it was as if he had no eyes at all, just two empty circles.

Here's what the thin-faced man said to the fat man: "What are you doing, Little Davy?"—this being the fat man's name.

"What does it look like?" said Little Davy, as his fingers tightened around Alex's neck.

"It looks like you're strangling that boy," said the thin man.

"Good on ya," said Little Davy with a laugh. "That's exactly what I'm doing."

"Take your hands off," said the thin-faced man. "You'll have time to strangle him later."

Alex gasped when Davy let go. Even though the fat man stood a foot away, his hands at his sides, Alex could still feel those sausage fingers around his neck.

"Ask him about the dingus," said the tall man, who, it became clear, was named Carl.

"Okay," said Little Davy, looking at Alex, "where is it?"

"Where's what?" asked Alex, as he tried to catch his breath.

"The dingus," said Davy.

"Who are you?" asked Alex.

"Never mind me," said Davy. "Just tell me how to find the dingus, or you'll get more like I already done."

"What's a dingus?" asked Alex, who was trying not to cry. In that moment, he thought fooling Ms. Reagan had been his biggest mistake ever. (He should have let her call the police.)

"Don't you understand?" said Little Davy. "If you don't tell me where you've got the dingus, I'll hurt you like before, but this time permanent."

"I don't know what you're talking about," said Alex. "What's a dingus?"

"The thingamajig," Little Davy shouted. "The device, the transporter, the time crosser, the dealio, the dingus!"

"What's happening?" Carl asked.

"The boy's playing deaf and dumb," said Little Davy. "He claims to know nothing of the dingus."

"All right, all right, this is not the place," Carl said. "Put him in the van."

Little Davy grabbed Alex by the arms and marched him toward the end of the alley. Alex knew this was the time to act. If they got him into the van, anything might happen. He punched and kicked, but it was no use. His feet kept moving toward the van.

Todd once told Alex something interesting. He said you shouldn't yell "help" when you need help. If you yell "help," people will run the other way, scared of whatever's scaring you.

"Then what should you yell?" Alex had asked.

"Yell 'fire.'"

"Why 'fire'?"

"Because everyone wants to see a fire."

So that's what Alex yelled as Little Davy pushed him down the alley.

*"Fire! Fire! Fire!"*

He yelled it so loudly and passionately that Davy himself was fooled. Letting go of Alex, he turned on his heel and, sounding like a three-year-old, asked, "Where's the fire? Where is it? Where?"

"There's no fire, you moron," shouted Carl. "You've been tricked. Just grab the boy."

But by this time, Alex had slipped away. When Davy turned to chase him, three or four people stood at the end of the alley. They had walked over from Park Avenue, hoping to see a fire. What they saw instead—a fat man with sausage fingers chasing a boy with a backpack as a van idled in the distance—concerned them, but not enough to stir them to action. Instead, they were dumbstruck, like deer in headlights.

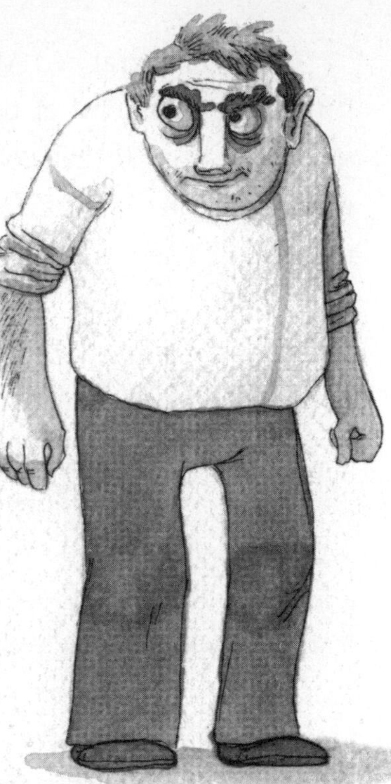

"Come on, Davy!" Carl shouted. "The setup stinks! We'll get the boy later."

"Or earlier," said Davy.

3

# CRAZY THINGS YOU FIND IN BOOKS

Alex sprinted home, racing past weekend athletes and marathon dads. It's funny. You put a jogger next to a kid running for his life, even if they're side by side, even if they're going the same speed, and you can tell the difference. It's something in the eyes, the difference between a practice and a game.

Alex spent the rest of the day watching TV with his brother. Sprawled on the couch, he looked like every other kid in the world, but he was all knots inside. Who were those men? he wondered. And what's a dingus?

He asked his brother.

"Tell you what," said Steven. "You keep your hands off my dingus, and I'll keep my hands off yours."

Alex snuck into his father's office. The computer was off. Next to it was a stack of paper, the book Mr. Trumble had been working on. At first, the stack had grown by leaps and bounds. In the last few months, however, progress had slowed to a crawl. Alex looked at the title page.

Here's what it said:

**THE BOOK ALEX TRUMBLE IS NOT SUPPOSED TO READ**

**by Dalton Trumble**

Alex opened the big dictionary his father kept near the window. He looked up the word *dingus* and read the definition: "Dingus: any unspecified or unspecifiable object; something one does not know the name of or does not wish to name."

Alex was quiet at dinner. He knew he should say something about what had happened outside the library—the situation might be dangerous not just to him, but to his entire family—but he did not. *Why?* Because what would he say? Two freaks cornered him in the alley by the candy store and demanded he give them the dingus? So when his mother asked, "What happened today?" he said, "Nothing," and when his father asked, "What did you do this morning?" he again said, "Nothing."

Alex's mother and father were not standard-issue parents. If you went to the store and asked for two everyday Americans, mother and father, a matching set, these are not the people you would get off the shelf. They seemed a little absent, in fact, and were not always around when Alex needed them. On the downside, this meant Alex sometimes felt like he was raising himself or was being raised by his brother, which was worse. On the upside, it gave him freedom, time to scheme and grow.

Besides, he knew his parents loved him. The bad things were just the reverse side of the things that made them great: his mother's obsession with work, with doing good in the world; his father's full-body immersion in stories, his life as a writer, which was the life of a dreamer, meaning he was often somewhere else even when he was sitting right in front of you. (I cannot be taken as an impartial judge of Dalton Trumble, for a reason that will become clear later.)

As the family ate takeout pizza, Mrs. Trumble talked about her latest case. "I have a new client, such a strange man," she told them. "This client—get this!—was found asleep at the scene of a crime. Just snoring away! There were two dead bodies at his side, and my client was curled up next to them. When the police woke him, and he was not easy to wake, he was confused. He didn't know where he was or how he got there. He remembered nothing, not even his name. The police are calling him Dimwitty, because they think he's a dimwit."

"What's a dimwit?" Steven asked.

"A dull bulb," said Mrs. Trumble. "But I don't agree. I think he's very smart, but something happened to him. Some trauma. If we could just find someone who knows his story."

"Why don't you call his mother?" asked Steven.

"We can't find his mother, or anyone related to him," said Mrs. Trumble. "Another weird thing: his wallet was filled with strange bills."

"Isn't money just money?" said Steven.

"Not this money. On the front were presidents no one has ever heard of, and on the back, where you'd normally see a picture of a building or something, there was a picture of a strange device, with mirrors and a beam of light. And the money was for funny amounts."

"Funny how?" asked Mr. Trumble as he folded a piece of pizza.

Mrs. Trumble explained. "Not twenties and tens and fives and ones. These bills were for nine dollars, eighteen and a half dollars, infinity dollars. And there really is something odd about this man," Mrs. Trumble added. "He strikes me as an important person who's

not important yet—a man who will be important, in some other country, at some other time. Does that sound crazy?"

"A little," said Mr. Trumble, smiling.

After dinner, Alex went to the top of the turret.

Here's what the bad men didn't know—Alex did not have the dingus, but he did have another copy of the book they had mutilated in the library. Over the past few months, Alex had painstakingly Xeroxed most of the book so he could study it at home when he was e-mailing Dr. Shaprut. He found page 567, which had been torn out of the library copy, and read the chapter title: "Vanishing Light, or How to Measure the Universe with a Fiddle String."

He skimmed a dozen pages that explained the nature of time, which the writer compared to a river. For the most part, you follow the river downstream, carried by the current, present to future. But with the right kind of engine, you could travel upstream, the way you came, back through time. Then, anticipating the work of Albert Einstein by fifty years, the writer said space is time and time is space. If you move through one, you move through the other. You cannot travel in space—climb the turret, walk into town—without also traveling in time. For most of us, that's one second into the future for every one second on the clock. But what if you could speed the passage of time? What if you could move into the future not at a rate of one second per second, but at a rate of two seconds per second, or two years per second? And might there also be a way to slow time, to move at the rate of a half second per second, or zero seconds per second, or to stop moving altogether, or even to move backward in time?

At the end of the chapter, the Buckskinned Philosopher said there was indeed a way to travel in time. If you built a device (a dingus, Alex said to himself) that warped space, you would warp time. A whirlpool of light would, for example, confuse space as a whirlpool of water confuses the current in a river. You'd get pulled into a whirlpool near the waterfall. A powerful tide would drag you under, then carry you against the current, ejecting you back upstream.

On the edge of the page, in the margin, the philosopher had written a string of numbers.

Alex bent close to examine them. He stared, then stared some more. Then, in a flash, he saw the pattern.

I won't go into detail, as I don't understand all the details myself, but I will say that, in these numbers, Alex spotted a solution to the problem of time travel, if only a few technical details could be worked out. Alex made his discovery with a shudder. Tingles went up and down his spine, and he felt dreamy and detached, as if he were running a high fever.

Above the numbers, the Buckskinned Philosopher had jotted down a poem, just a few lines, which, according to Dr. Shaprut (Alex immediately e-mailed her after he made his discovery), had actually been written by Li Po, a great poet who lived in China over a thousand years ago. Dr. Shaprut said this was clearly the philosopher's favorite work of literature, as he had written it in other places in the book. "It's about forgetting your problems and quirks to such a degree that you become one with nature, thus disappear," she explained.

*The birds have vanished into the sky.*
*Now the last cloud drains away.*
*We sit together, the mountain and me,*
*until only the mountain remains.*

When Alex read the poem again late that night, he seemed to find a second, secret meaning:

*We sit together, the mountain and me,*
*until only the mountain remains.*

It wasn't that the poet, forgetting himself, made his ego vanish. It was that the poet, using the ideas contained in the string of numbers, opened a hole in time and made his entire body disappear. The more Alex thought about it, the more certain he was that this was no mere theory. That it had happened. That the poet had traveled via wormhole from eighth-century China to nineteenth-century America. The Buckskinned Philosopher was none other than Li Po. With this in mind, still feeling feverish, Alex went through the book, discovering clues, bits of ancient wisdom, and poetry everywhere in the pages.

"And I can go the same way as Li Po, and follow the same path, and enter the same door, if only I can solve the mechanical problem."

As Alex was telling himself this, the solution to that problem presented itself. Or, more accurately, he had already seen the solution, but now, for the first time, he recognized the significance of what he had seen.

It was in a joke book, of all places, that his brother had given him on his birthday. There were tricks and pranks to play on your friends, but in the back there was something odd and interesting. Alex looked through his shelves until he found the book. It was called *The Ha Has, the Hee Hees, and the Oh Nose!*

On the last page, under a picture of four mirrors and a beam of light, the authors—two elderly men—explained how, if you arranged the mirrors in a square so that each bounced a light beam onto the next, like relay runners passing a baton, the light would get moving from mirror to mirror, around the square, at an astounding speed. This would create a vortex, a whirlpool of light.

There was no mention of warps or time travel, but Alex figured that was because the writers themselves did not know the implications of their own trick. To these guys, the mirrors and the light were merely a way to create rainbow shimmers and impress your friends. But if put together the right way, with the Buckskinned

Philosopher's string of numbers in mind, Alex believed he could create the kind of trick that would really impress his friends—take them back to see the world before they were born.

4

# INTO THE WOODS

The next day was a Monday, and it was busy. There was a test, a paper to write, and an assembly where the world's greatest yo-yo team showed off its skills.

Alex didn't talk to Todd till lunch. They sat in a corner of the lunchroom, but it was impossible to speak. Every time Alex got started, another kid came over with a question, a joke, or just to hang around the stars of the school.

You might be wondering why Alex Trumble was admired by his classmates. He wasn't the sort of kid who usually sits atop the social whirl. But he was touched by a kind of freak intelligence—the ability to see every number on a page as one image, the way most people see an eye, an ear, and a mouth as a face. It was the sort of intelligence that usually separates a kid from his classmates. The thing that makes him special also makes him seem weird.

Alex didn't have this problem. For whatever reason, his gift made him confident, which made everyone comfortable around him. He was like the great ball player who raises the level of all the other players on the field—who makes the good player excellent, the mediocre player good, and even the lousy player decent.

As a result, Alex's table at lunch became a kind of courtroom, where kids, even seventh- and eighth-graders, came to have questions answered and debates settled. Take, for example, the case of *stupid* versus *dumb*. In the midst of a fight, the cause of which was soon forgotten, one kid had called another kid dumb, and the second shot back, "I might be dumb, but you're stupid."

This led to a debate on the nature of stupidity versus dumbness. Was there a difference? If so, what? And which is worse?

This fight, which replaced the first, almost came to

blows before someone said, "Hey, it's lunchtime. Trumble's in session. Let's get him to settle it."

"Yes," said Alex. "There is a difference between stupid and dumb. *Dumb* means you know nothing and act like you know nothing. *Stupid* means you know nothing but act like you know something."

"But which is worse?" asked one of the kids.

"Wow, that's a stupid question," said Alex.

All the kids laughed and the argument was forgotten. In this way, Alex showed he understood not only words and facts but people and moods. It was the secret of his success.

Which is why Alex and Todd did not get a chance to speak until the second bell had rung, meaning lunch was definitely over. They talked in the hall as they hurried back to class. Alex had a lot to say and not much time. After school, the Trumbles were leaving for their yearly trip to the North Woods of Wisconsin. They stayed in a cabin at Camp Cherokee, in Eagle River, where Dalton Trumble had spent his summers as a boy.

"I wish I wasn't going up to camp this weekend," said Alex.

"Come on," Todd said. "It'll be fun."

When Alex finally did tell Todd about the library and the men, Little Davy and Carl, the white van, the old book, the beam of light, Todd was floored.

Here's all he could manage to say: "So the yelling 'fire' thing worked?"

"Yeah," said Alex. "It saved my life."

Todd was quiet a moment. Then, in a soft voice, a whisper, he said, "I think you're getting in too deep. It sounds dangerous. Like big-time dangerous."

"Yeah, but I'm in the middle," Alex said with a shrug. "It's happening."

Todd took an old baseball card out of his shirt pocket and handed it to Alex. "Hold on to it while you're up at camp," he said. "It might come in handy."

"You can't give me your lucky card," Alex said. "You have a game this weekend."

"Just take it."

Alex examined the card. Bent and hard used, it showed Mark Grace, who played for the Chicago Cubs a thousand years ago, standing at first base in Wrigley Field. This was Todd's favorite player. "Because he never looked like

he was trying, even when he really was," he explained. On the back, next to the statistics, Todd had written a few notes to himself, which he always recited in his head as he stood in the on-deck circle: *elbow up, weight back, eyes on the ball.*

"You need it," Alex said.

"Yeah, but you need it more."

# 5

# THE GREATEST DOG IN THE WORLD

Alex had a dog. Did I tell you that? Well, it's my mistake if I didn't. Because the dog was important. After his family and his best friend, Alex loved his dog most of all.

Each day, when Alex got home from school, his dog was waiting, chest out, tail wagging—the ready position of all hero canines. The dog had a white body with black spots, like a cow. Her eyes were brown and set far apart. When there was food on the table, they became soft and dreamy. But if a stranger crossed the lawn, they became hard and mean.

Her head was big for her body, and her paws were

big for her legs. She was always up to something. She used to run away, be gone for hours, then return covered in brambles or chewing a piece of gum. Once, when the neighbors had a party, she snuck in behind a guest and ate all the mini hot dogs. Mr. Wagner—that was the man who lived next door—called and shouted into the phone, "Can someone please get Scout? This is a gosh-darn travesty!"

That was her name, by the way. Scout. She had tremendous personality and was really a wonderful dog.

To stop her from wandering, Mr. Trumble had her fitted with an electric dog collar. There was a square gray box hooked to the collar like a trinket. Two rubber-tipped steel prongs dug into the fur on Scout's neck. If she got near the property line, the box started to beep. If she stayed there for three seconds, a shock was delivered through those rubber-tipped prongs. It seemed nasty to Alex—Scout was, by nature, a wanderer, a dog with an almost human spirit—but Mr. Trumble asked his son, "Would you rather she get a little shock now and then, or get hit by a car?"

Alex used to imagine fitting his brother with an electric collar. This would keep him out of the turret, certain parts of the yard, and Alex's room. If his father complained, Alex would say, "Would you rather Steven get a little shock now and then, or get hit by my fist?"

As Alex walked up the driveway, Scout fell in beside him, just a boy and his dog. Alex's father was loading the sleeping bags and other gear into the trunk of the car. For a moment, as Alex crossed the yard, he thought he saw a face in the window of the turret, a familiar face, looking down at him, but a moment later, the face was gone.

Alex dropped his backpack in the kitchen and ran to his room, Scout behind him the whole way. He went on to his computer, looked at his e-mail and the sports scores, then, before he knew it, an hour had passed. His father called up from the driveway. It was time to go.

The Trumbles drove a Jeep Wagoneer, red with fake wood paneling. On most trips, Mr. Trumble drove and Mrs. Trumble sat next to him, with the boys in back and Scout between them, her head on Alex's knee.

The family was on the road all afternoon and into the night, but Alex never got bored. There was always something to look at. There was the highway speeding past, all those people in all those cars. There were, once they crossed into Wisconsin, custard stands and fireworks shacks. There were lakes, beautiful and inky black between the trees. There were diners and motels, each with its neon vacancy sign.

The woods crowded close on either side of the road until it felt like the car was zooming through a tunnel of pine. At nine P.M., they turned off the main road onto the grounds of Cherokee. The camp was a few dozen cabins on a green hill above a lake, with forest on either side. A main hall, a mess hall, an infirmary, an equipment shed, docks, and fishing boats filled the grounds.

It was family week, when former campers and their children visited. Before the Trumbles carried their gear into cabin nine, they went into the main hall to say hello to friends. Mr. Trumble knew everyone. Steven had friends, too, but Alex spent most of his time alone in the woods.

When the Trumbles got into their cabin, Mr. Trumble discovered they were short a sleeping bag. "Darn it," he said. "I bet it's just sitting in the garage with nothing to do." Alex volunteered to sleep without a bag, making himself a nest of pillows and wool blankets.

If you think it's quiet in the woods, you're wrong.

Between the hours of midnight and four A.M., the forest rings like a symphony, with each animal, bug, bird, and critter playing its horn—the peepers, the hoot owls, the locusts. If you think it's dark in the woods, you're wrong about that, too. Well, yes, it's dark on the ground—you can't see your hand in front of your face—but the sky is ablaze with light. There are comets and meteors and red giants and blue dwarfs. There are points of singularity, where entire universes have been compacted to the size of a dot.

Alex had a terrible dream.

It was morning in the dream, and the sun was white. Alex was sitting on the floor of the cabin, looking at the baseball card Todd had given him. It began to multiply. What had been one card became two, ten, a million. He was buried in cards. He ran out, leaving his family asleep, careful to not let the screen door slam.

He headed for the woods and was soon walking up and down hills, with the lake on his right, then on his left, then behind him. He saw snakes in the woods and small animals. He heard voices. Then he saw his brother, only now his brother was older, a grown man, as if many years had gone by. And though Alex walked ahead the whole time, he soon found himself back at the cabin.

Had he walked in a circle?

He burst through the screen door, not worrying about the noise. He wanted to wake his family, but there was no one to wake. The cabin was deserted. Cobwebs in the corners. His mother came in, and she cried.

"Where have you been?" she asked.

"I went for a walk."

"That was an awfully long walk."

"I was gone for less than an hour."

"You've been gone for thirty-five years."

Alex looked at his mother closely. She was an old woman, wrinkled and gray. He looked at his own hands. They were meaty, cracked, and weathered, the hands of a middle-aged man.

"Where are we?" Alex asked.

"In Eagle River," said Mrs. Trumble. "You're on trial for murder."

Alex woke in a sweat, sitting up on his cot as reveille blared, calling the campers to the parade ground, where a dozen families stood as the flag was raised.

It had just been a dream, he told himself, but the dread lingered and made him feel detached, like everything that was happening had happened before and would happen again.

He walked to the mess hall in a daze, then went to the waterfront, where plans were made for the day. He spent the morning with his father, fishing for pike. Everyone split up in the afternoon. Mr. and Mrs.

Trumble went to play tennis. Steven went with his friend Zeke Anderson, a short, muscular kid with jug ears. Mrs. Trumble suggested Alex go with Steven and Zeke, but Steven stammered and said, "Uh, yeah, well, I understand, but the thing is, me and, uh, Zeke plan to goof around in the woods—"

"That's okay," Alex said before his mother could protest. "I want to take Scout out to the fields to play fetch anyway."

As so often happens, this one little decision would prove crucial.

6

# THE CASE OF THE DISAPPEARING BROTHER

This is the part of the story it hurts me to write. I have been dreading it since I sat down to make this account. Writing about events like this, vanishing children and traumatized families, is not among my favorite things.

Of course, I have no choice.

The story is the story.

At 4:32 that afternoon, Zeke Anderson ran out of the woods. He raced across the fields, past the tether-ball court, past the mess hall and infirmary to the cabins, where Mr. and Mrs. Trumble were sitting on lawn chairs.

Zeke was breathing hard as he came, shouting "Help! Help! Help!"

"What! What is it?" asked Mrs. Trumble, jumping to her feet.

"It's Steven," said Zeke.

"What about Steven?" asked Mr. Trumble.

"Two men grabbed him in the woods."

"What do you mean?" asked Mr. Trumble.

(*Asked* is too soft a word. It was more of a shriek.)

"They pushed him into a car, a white van, and took him away," said Zeke.

"What? Who? Why?"

This was Mr. Trumble, and he was trying to stay calm, even thinking to himself, "Stay calm," but his face had turned a deathly pale.

"At the end of Old Counselors Road," said Zeke. "These men came out of nowhere and grabbed Steven."

"Call the police," Mr. Trumble shouted to no one and everyone. Then, turning to Zeke, he said, "Take us there."

Zeke and Mr. and Mrs. Trumble ran across the fields, joined by a handful of friends. Alex was at the back of the crowd, Scout on his heels.

Old Counselors Road had once been the main

entrance to camp, but it was replaced years ago when the highway was completed. It had since been allowed to grow over with grapevine and weeds and had become a path twisting through the trees. The branches met overhead in a canopy. Even when the sun was high, it was dark and gloomy on the road.

Zeke stood in the leaves, explaining how Steven had been taken. A police cruiser rolled up as Zeke was talking. The cops parked on the shoulder, red and blue lights flashing. The two cops asked Zeke to start again, from the beginning.

"We were standing here, in this exact spot, talking, doing nothing, when the van came from nowhere," said Zeke.

"What do you mean, 'from nowhere'?" asked Cop One.

"It wasn't there, then it was," said Zeke.

"What direction did it come from?" asked Cop Two.

"That's just it," said Zeke. "It came from no direction. It just appeared."

"Then what happened?" asked the first cop, opening his notebook.

"This ugly fat man got out and started yelling at us," said Zeke.

Little Davy, Alex thought.

"Then what?" asked Cop Two.

"We tried to run," said Zeke, "but the fat man caught Steven and pushed him into the van."

"Why didn't he take you?" asked Mr. Trumble.

"I don't know," said Zeke. "It's like he didn't even notice me."

"What direction did the van go?" asked Cop One.

"They started that way," Zeke said, pointing up the road, "then something funny happened. They started that way, but they didn't go that way."

"Did they turn around?" asked Cop Two.

"No," said Zeke, "they disappeared."

"Disappeared? How?" asked Mr. Trumble, whose tone was controlled fury.

"The van had funny headlights," said Zeke. "They were like search beams, and there were four of them, and as the van started to move, the beams started to spin, and they made a pool of light, and the van drove into the pool of light and disappeared."

Here's what Alex heard Cop One whisper to Cop Two: "This kid is useless."

"Please tell me this is a joke," said Mrs. Trumble.

Alex could hear the stress in his mother's voice and see tears in the corners of her eyes. "Are you and Steven playing a trick? Is he hiding?"

"I'm telling the truth," said Zeke.

"WHERE IS HE?" Mr. Trumble shouted.

"The men in the van took him away," said Zeke.

Alex felt something tugging at his pants. He looked down. It was Scout. She was telling him something, or trying to. Alex followed her across the road. She pawed at a piece of paper caught in the spiky limbs of a raspberry bush. "Thanks, girl," Alex said, bending down to examine the clue. It was a baseball card. And not just any baseball card. It was the card Todd had given him: Mark Grace in the sunshine of Wrigley Field.

Alex turned it over to study the reverse side, where, next to the statistics, he saw, in the familiar handwriting of his friend, Todd's on-deck mantra, *elbow up, weight back, eyes on the ball.*

For a moment, it seemed obvious what must've happened. Steven had swiped the card from Alex's pocket, brought it here, and thrown it away or lost it in the struggle. But when Alex checked his pocket—he generally wore the same pants for days on end, until they could probably stand up and walk away on their own—he found the card there, too. The very same card. *What the . . . ? How in the . . . ? What in the name of . . . ?* He was baffled. Now he had two cards that were exactly the same. He thought about this for a moment, then slid both cards into his pants pocket and followed the crowd, which was hurrying back to camp.

The Trumbles were met at cabin nine by two law enforcement officers, men clearly more important than those who had questioned Zeke on Old

Counselors Road. Two hours had passed since the disappearance. These officers worked for the FBI, the police for the whole country. They wore black suits and black ties—that's how you could tell they were more important. At some point, they questioned Alex. He did a lot of talking but didn't tell them everything he knew. His parents were with him, but seemed far off, removed. One of the men took notes, while the other patted Alex on the shoulder and told him, "There, there, it's okay to cry."

The men then asked Alex's mother if they could speak to her alone. She led them to the mess hall. Alex followed, then hid in the kitchen, where he could hear everything. Most of the questions were not about Steven, or Zeke, or Old Counselors Road. They were about Mrs. Trumble's mysterious client, the man the police called Dimwitty. The FBI wanted to know where he'd really come from and if Mrs. Trumble truly believed him to be innocent.

Mrs. Trumble was patient and answered their questions, but she finally got angry and demanded, "Why are you asking about my client? Did my work bring this trouble on my family?" She shuddered to herself as she said this.

"We think the cases might be connected," one of the agents said calmly.

"How?" asked Mrs. Trumble, leaning forward in her chair.

"A witness has come forward in the Dimwitty case," the agent said, and now both of the officers were standing. "Just before the police arrived, a white van was spotted, then it just disappeared."

Mrs. Trumble fell back into her chair and sobbed.

# 7

# TROUBLE IS MY BUSINESS

You know how it is in a bad dream, when there is no sense of time, and you never know where you are, and anything can follow anything, and you can't wake up no matter how hard you try?

That's what life was like for the Trumbles after Steven was kidnapped. The family stayed in Eagle River for several weeks, hoping Steven would just walk through the door one afternoon, but he never did. Perhaps the Trumbles should have gone home so Alex could attend school, but they were not thinking rationally.

The family checked into a motel in town. There was a swimming pool, but Alex never went near it. Is there anything sadder than a motel pool with no one swimming in it? A machine in the lobby sold soda and candy. There was a nice woman at the front desk, who, like everyone in Eagle River, seemed to know everything that had befallen the Trumbles.

Each morning, the family made a pilgrimage to Old Counselors Road. They stood and listened and waited for a clue, but no clue was offered. It was just woods and silence out there, the sun shining through the leaves in golden search beams. Each afternoon, they went to the police station to ask if any progress had been made in the investigation. None ever had. After Alex missed almost a month of school and it seemed like nothing more could be done in the woods, the family, what was left of it, went back to Illinois.

Alex felt like he had disappeared, too. Or his parents had. It was just the boy and the dog and the house now. His mother and father had gone into another dimension, behind a screen of grief. They could be seen and observed but neither spoken to nor reached.

STEVEN

One day Alex crept into his father's office and looked at the pages stacked on the desk next to the computer. *What would become of the book now?* Mr. Trumble had stopped writing when Steven disappeared. The book stood forlorn, like a half-built house or a half-cooked meal.

Alex read the first few chapters. The pages seemed eerily familiar. Reading them was like looking through a window at his own life. Alex was in them, and so were Steven and Mrs. Trumble, and her client with the funny money. Todd Johnston was in them, too, and Scout, bounding and sniffing. The story was interesting but incomplete, frozen, because, with the disappearance of Steven, time for the Trumble family was itself frozen. Mr. Trumble stopped, so the people in the story stopped—the clock reached a certain hour, then stayed there.

"I'll fix everything," Alex told himself.

With this in mind, Alex kept reading about wormholes and time machines, plotting and planning. He had never been more busy than he was during those terrible days. There has to be an answer, he thought, a solution to the riddle of the men and the van, the pool of light at the end of Old Counselors Road. If he could solve the riddle, he could turn back the clock. If he could turn back the clock, he could rescue his brother. If he could rescue his brother, he could save his family.

# 8

# A GOOD REASON TO TIME TRAVEL

When Alex returned to school, news of the Trumbles' disaster was everywhere. Teachers did not call on him that first day, or, if they did, it was to answer the easiest question or share his feelings. He hated all the caring concern. It was like a pillow pushed over his face. He couldn't breathe.

Todd was the only person Alex could really talk to. He spent lunch with Todd and stood with him in the hall between classes. He told Todd everything that had happened, what it was like and how it felt, then said, "But I know I can fix it."

Todd looked at Alex with surprise, the way you might look at a crazy man.

"How?"

"By building a time machine," said Alex, "and using it to go back to Cherokee on the day my brother was taken, and stopping him from getting in that van."

Todd slapped himself on the forehead.

"What?" said Alex.

"You sound nuts."

"I'm not nuts," Alex said, irritated. "I figured it out. That's why Little Davy and Carl ripped the pages from that book. Because the answer was there. They were trying to keep the secret to themselves. And they came to stop me from building a time machine."

"But why do they care if you build a time machine?"

"I don't know," Alex said. "I have to build a time machine to find out."

"You have to build a time machine to find out why you have to build a time machine?"

"Yeah," said Alex.

"Like I said, you sound crazy."

"You want proof?" asked Alex.

"Sure."

Alex pulled the baseball cards out of his pocket: Todd's lucky card and the card Scout had uncovered in the woods.

Todd examined them side by side, confused, then said, "I don't get it. Did you make a copy?"

"No," said Alex, "it's not a copy. There's only one card, but it looks like two. It's the same card from different places in time."

"You lost me."

"Imagine you had two TVs side by side, and both of them were showing the first Harry Potter movie, but on one TV, the movie was just starting and Harry didn't know his true identity or anything, but on the other, the movie was nearly over and Harry knew who he was and what he had to do. Would you say the older Harry was just a copy, or would you say they were actually the same Harry?"

"The same. But these are baseball cards. You can't ask them questions or prove any of this."

"I think I can," Alex said.

"How?"

"If I'm right and you rip the first card, the tear will appear on the second card."

Todd made a small rip in the corner of his lucky card. A moment later, the rip appeared on the second card. Todd shivered. But when he tried to repeat the trick by tearing the second card, nothing happened to the first.

"Why didn't it rip?"

"Because this card comes later," said Alex, grabbing the second card. "This card is the future, and this card is the past. What happens in the past affects the future. But what happens in the future cannot affect the past." Alex smiled. It was a sly smile. "Unless, of course . . ."

"Unless, of course, what?"

"Unless, of course, you build a time machine."

"What are you saying? That my lucky card built a dingus and went back in time?"

"No," Alex said, "a person built the dingus, and it was this person who carried your card back in time."

"And this person is?"

"Me," Alex said.

"Alex, you're really smart and all, but this is insane."

"Think about it," said Alex. "Who had the card? Me. Who wants to go back up to Eagle River to save his family? Me. It makes perfect sense. I build the machine, go back to Eagle River, then leave the card at the end of Old Counselors Road for me to find. It's a message from myself to myself."

"Saying what?" asked Todd.

"Saying yes, you can build a time machine, and to prove it, here's a baseball card from the future: now hurry up and build the machine; your family depends on it."

9

# LET'S LIGHT THIS CANDLE

First order of business was supplies, the things Alex needed to build the dingus. This was based on his own design for the machine, which he had carefully drawn on a piece of graph paper. Each piece of equipment was chosen with a specific task in mind. He took the list out of his pocket and read it to Todd, who still did not fully believe but had come along to help anyway. The friends were sitting in the turret, Scout between them.

"Four mirrors to bounce the light," said Alex. "And they have to be small, clear mirrors, like the kind my father uses when he's shaving."

"Easy," said Todd. "What else?"

"A flashlight with a narrow beam, or, better, a laser pointer, one of those things that looks like a pen and throws a red light all over the place. That's going to give us the kind of focused beam we need. Duct tape, glue, electrical wire, a tape measure, and an iPod."

"That's it?" said Todd. "That's all you need to make a time machine?"

"I think so," said Alex, checking his list. "Oh, yeah, and lemonade."

"Why?"

"Because we're gonna get thirsty."

Alex and Todd spent the rest of the day searching and gathering. They found two mirrors among Mr. Trumble's bathroom stuff and two more in Mrs. Trumble's makeup. They found duct tape, glue, a tape measure, and electrical wire in the garage. They found a laser pointer in Mrs. Trumble's briefcase. She used it when arguing a case in court. For a long time, they couldn't find an iPod or figure out where to get one. Then Alex remembered that Steven had an iPod in his room.

"So we take it?" asked Todd.

"Yup," said Alex.

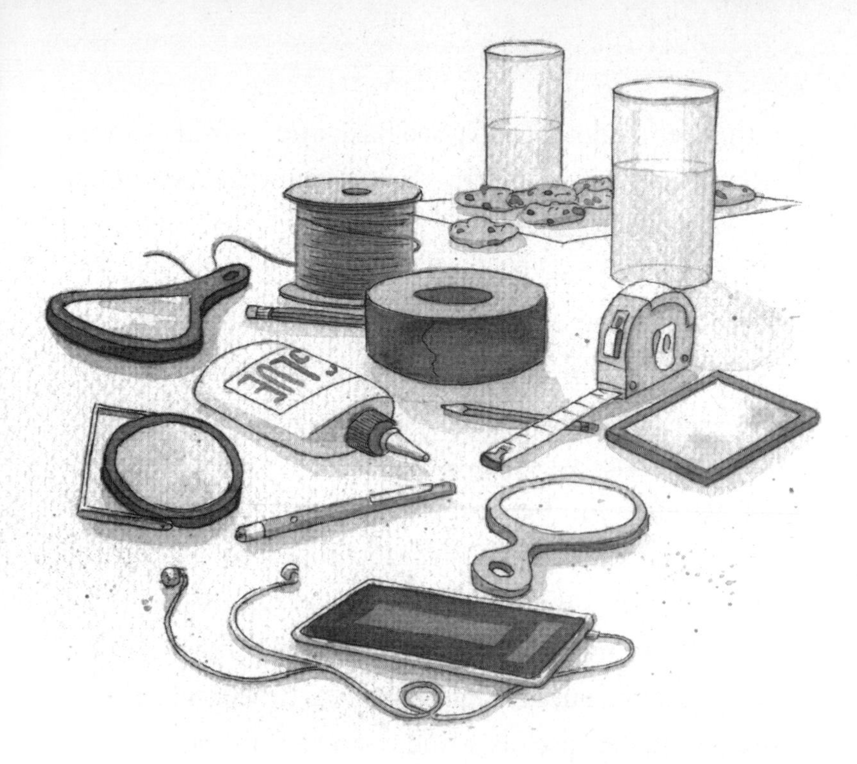


Todd and Alex did all this gathering unnoticed, as the adults in the house were lost in their grief. After dinner, which consisted of cookies and the already mentioned lemonade, the boys started assembling the machine. They decided to build it at the top of the turret, near the big windows that faced the lake. There were two wooden posts up there—four feet apart—which would serve as the threshold of the machine. Using the tape measure, Alex marked out a perfect square, four feet by four feet, indicating each corner with a pencil dot. He stepped back and looked—it was just air now, but when finished, it would be, he hoped, a door into another time.

He wound four loops of double-stick duct tape and stuck a loop on each pencil dot—the four corners of the square. He pressed a mirror into each loop. They sat a quarter inch or so off the wooden posts, meaning they could be twisted and turned. Then, referring to the string of numbers on page 601 in *Light Beams and Indians*, he made a series of tiny adjustments, the details of which I will not reveal here, in part because I don't want any overly curious readers following Alex through time, upsetting the space-time continuum, and partly because, as I said, I don't fully understand the details myself.

Alex fiddled with the mirrors until each one faced the mirror next to it, which made a chain of reflection. If you looked into one mirror, your face would be reflected from mirror to mirror around the square. Even if you stepped away, your reflection would continue to spin around the circuit.

Alex explained the machine as he worked. When adults explain something that's complicated, you end up feeling stupid; when Alex explained a complicated thing, you ended up feeling smart. "According to Einstein, time and space are the same thing," he told Todd. "Now, think what that means. If you take a shortcut across space, you take a shortcut across time. And that's all a time warp is: a shortcut, just like a tunnel through a mountain. Why climb over the mountain when you can tunnel through and reach the same spot on the far side using half the number of steps?"

"Pretend I understand," said Todd. "But how do you actually warp space?"

Todd always asked good questions—he cut to the core issues, just like that.

"With the laser pointer," said Alex. "You aim the laser at the mirrors and get the red light spinning around the square, faster and faster. After a while, the space between the mirrors will get stirred up by the light and it will begin to warp. You won't be able to see it, but it will be happening. That empty space will turn and turn until it becomes a whirlpool. If you step into the whirlpool, you'll come out in another time."

"Like the tunnel through a mountain," said Todd.

"Exactly," said Alex.

Alex's time machine would, in other words, be less rocket than boring machine, like one of those big trucks you see screw-driving deep into the earth, digging tunnels for subway trains or piping. It would make a wormhole, a tunnel through time and space.

"Even if it works," said Todd, "how do you control where it takes you? How do you know if you're going forward or back, or what year you'll be in when you come out? It'd be like jumping into a time well. You'd have to be crazy."

"That's what the iPod is for," Alex said. "I'm going to wire it to the machine, and it will control the tilt of the mirrors. The steeper the tilt, the faster the light moves around the square. The faster the light moves, the more severe the time warp. The more severe the time warp, the further you travel."

"How do you know if you're going into the future or into the past?"

"It's like a clock," said Alex. "If light travels around the square clockwise, you go into the future. If it travels counterclockwise, you go into the past."

"What about getting home, back to our own time? Have you thought about that?"

"Of course," said Alex, sitting in a chair now, working with the iPod and electrical wire. "I don't want to take any permanent trips. This isn't a machine that flies like a plane. It's a tunnel. You type in your destination using the keypad. Not where you want to go, but when you want to arrive. Year, day, hour, minute, second. The forward end of the tunnel should open into that exact moment while the near end stays right here in this room. To get home, you just go back through the tunnel."

"Yeah, but how do you know where you'll land? I mean, what if you wind up in the wrong town, or in the middle of the ocean?"

"You're not getting it," said Alex. "You don't travel in *space*—only in time. You never go anywhere. You stay in the same place while traveling to a different time. The other side of the tunnel is always here, only it opens into an earlier or a later moment. You enter here and you exit here—same spot, same room, same everything."

Alex paused, then said, "Unless, of course, the house is gone, or the lake has overflowed and filled the town. Then you might have a problem. Otherwise, you never leave the room. Just zoom ahead or zoom back."

Todd thought a moment, said "Oh," smiled, then said "Oh" again, only in an entirely different way.

This is what it sounded like the second time: "Ohhhhhhhhh!" Todd's smile quickly turned to a frown. "What if someone comes in here while you're time traveling and shuts off the machine?"

"No worries. Each side will stay where you left it. It will look like a jumble of old mirrors until someone turns it back on."

"Can you turn it on from either side?"

"If it works like I think it will," said Alex, "it'll be like the baseball card. The same door standing in two separate moments in time."

Then, working together for three, maybe four hours, Todd and Alex finished the machine. By nine P.M., everything was in place: the four mirrors, the iPod, everything.

Todd stood back, thrilled. "Let's call the laser pointer 'the candle.'"

"Why?" Alex asked.

"Because then, when we're ready to go, we can say 'Light the candle,' the way the engineers do when they launch a rocket into space."

"All right," said Alex. "Light the candle."

"Just like that?" asked Todd.

"Hold on," said Alex.

He held a sheet of paper in front of the mirrors, where the reflection of his face was still circulating, faster and faster. Alex called this "cleaning the square."

Stepping back, he said, "Light the candle."

Todd handed Alex the laser pointer. Alex aimed it. When the light hit the first mirror, it began to travel, mirror to mirror, around the square.

"What happens now?" asked Todd.

"We wait," said Alex, sitting against the wall, ten feet from the machine.

"Wait for what?"

"For the beam to get up to speed and space to warp."

They sat for twenty minutes, mesmerized by the machine.

As the light gained speed, they could actually see it. No longer a dot, it became a solid beam, a glowing line pulsating around the square. Now and then, the space inside the square turned hazy and, for a moment, looking at the lake through the square was like looking at the same scene at a different hour, a different time of day. On the left and right, the lake had faded to deep blue and reflected the setting sun. But the lake was bright inside the square and the sun was still high overhead, as if two pictures taken at different moments had been spliced together. Then the floor shuddered and the machine groaned and the scene inside the square again matched the scene outside.

Alex got to his feet.

"What now?" Todd asked.

"Let's test it."

The test was simple. Alex had a stack of pennies, which he tossed, one at a time, into the square. If the machine was working, the pennies would vanish, meaning they had gone through the tunnel into another time. But the pennies didn't vanish. They instead flew through the air and clanged harmlessly off the window on the far side of the machine. One penny did seem to hesitate, waver, appear, and disappear, but then it, too, clanged off the glass across the room.

Todd didn't say anything. He didn't have to. Alex went over, head down, and held a sheet of paper in front of the mirrors, shutting off the machine. He sat on the ground. His face was wet with tears, but he choked back the sobs. Failure would mean the situation with his family—brother gone, parents destroyed—was his life forever. There would be no rescue, no solution.

Todd looked at his friend, but said nothing.

Sometimes crying is the best thing to do—for a little while, anyway.

After a few minutes, Todd quietly asked, "What're you going to do now?"

"I'm going to think," said Alex.

Todd smiled sadly and squeezed Alex's arm just above the right elbow.

"Don't worry. We'll figure something out."

# 10

# PARADISE ALLEY

"Where did I blow it?" Alex kept asking himself.

He had gone back to the books and filled pages with numbers, but could not find the answer. He skipped several days of school. All he wanted to do was sit and think. On some nights, he wrote long e-mails to Dr. Shaprut. He wanted to tell her what had happened, what he found, and where he was stuck. He stared and stared at these messages without pressing Send. He remembered his mother telling him about prosecutions in which the government intercepted and read a fugitive's e-mail.

What if Carl and Little Davy read my e-mail? he

asked himself. Won't this letter convince those jerks that I'm working on the dingus?

In the end, he always hit Delete, and this made him feel like a fugitive himself, the only person on a lonely planet.

Then, late one night, as he was at his desk, he heard a tap on his window, a pebble clinking off the glass. Then another. He opened the blind and looked out.

Todd was out there in the dark, calling up, "Come down! We need to talk."

Alex pulled on some clothes and headed outside. They walked in the backyard, Scout sniffing the grass behind them. "What's this garbage, skipping school, shutting yourself in like a lunatic?" Todd asked.

"I can't figure out where we went wrong," said Alex. "It's making me nuts."

"If you'd come to school, I could've told you where we went wrong."

"But you don't believe it's even possible."

"I didn't at first, but you changed my mind," Todd said. "Did you see that penny, how it sort of wavered, appeared and disappeared? We were close!"

"I know," said Alex, "but how do we get over the hump?"

"It's like my dad says: if a little doesn't work, how about a lot?"

"A lot of what?" asked Alex.

"Power," said Todd. "The machine's like a car. It looks cool on the outside, but the engine is too small. That's where I can help. You're good at numbers and big stuff, but when it comes to get up and go, you head to the Johnston house."

The Johnstons lived in a ramshackle house on the west side of town, as far as you could get from the lake and still call it Glencoe. To get there, the friends walked through deserted streets, then cut across subdivisions, where house was followed by identical house, where every blind was drawn and every light was out.

The Johnston house was dark, too, but there was a dirt lane behind the house, and it was full of life. This lane was bounded by garages, each with its door open, revealing another grease monkey working after hours on his or her dream machine. To locals, this stretch of late-night car-building activity was known as Paradise Alley.

Alex was in awe of the Johnstons' garage, this cathedral, where Todd's big sister, Frankie (she must've been seventeen) worked on her cars. Her great love was vintage automobiles. Frankie was tall and blond with big brown eyes, honestly the most beautiful person Alex had ever seen.

Mr. Johnston, who was a part-time race car driver—he ran Frankie's creations at a track on the edge of the city—and a full-time carpenter, got Frankie started and taught her everything he knew, but Frankie had gone way past him. "Just look at her," he would say, as his daughter put the last touches on an engine block or a crankshaft. "She's truly an artist!"

Vintage cars were the mania of Paradise Alley. You could hear engines turning over up and down the lane; cheers went up whenever some theory had finally been proven. It was, in fact, the perfect place for Alex to bring his problem. While he dealt with the abstract and the hardly believable, the denizens of the alley were mechanics—they lived on the ground, where an engine could always be made to go a little faster or drive a little harder.

When Todd and Alex came in the side door of the garage, Frankie was putting the last bolt on an orange '66 Pontiac GTO, "an antique sunset driven by a rocket engine," she said, smiling. Mr. Johnston showed up a

few minutes later. He was tall with a big blond mustache, a broad smile, and big arms covered in sunspots and freckles. At first, he was worried about Alex, why he was out so late, did his parents know, and so on, but soon, like his daughter, he got caught up in Alex's problem, which was explained to them in a general way—a laser pointer, an iPod—with no mention of time travel.

When Mr. Jackson asked what the machine was for, Alex spoke two magic words: SCIENCE FAIR, which caused the benevolent blond-haired man's eyes to glaze over. From then on, he dealt with Alex's problem in the abstract manner of a physicist dealing with quantum mechanics.

"This computer—this iPod or whatever—you say it needs a kick in the pants?" Frankie finally asked.

"Yeah," said Alex.

"Computers are not my thing," said Frankie, "but I bet one of the boys can help."

She stuck two fingers under her tongue and whistled. In a moment, the garage was filled with the toughest kids in town, neighborhood legends who had dropped out of school or vanished altogether. They wore dirty tank tops under one-piece jumpsuits. They gathered around a cast-off old dining room table like the knights of King Arthur's court, drinking soda and analyzing.

In the end, it was a kid named Psycho who came up with a solution. Unlike the others, Psycho was into modern cars, imports from Japan, and had therefore come to know the ins and outs of the computer systems that controlled such cars. In an effort to get more out of his Toyota, or, as he explained it, "to get fifteen pounds into a ten-pound sack," Psycho had created a device he called the hand wringer. Through a series of computer tricks and default skips, Psycho's hand wringer would multiply the power of a Corolla five hundredfold.

He ran down the alley and came back with the device. It was half the size of a Coke can, a cylinder, dinged up and gray, with wires coming out the bottom.

"You open the iPod," Psycho said, "and connect these wires into the cables that lead to the battery. Then stand back, 'cuz that sucker's gonna cook."

"And I can just have it?" Alex asked.

"Sure," said Psycho, smiling, and now Alex could see that Psycho, who was small and intense, was missing a few teeth. "Any friend of Frankie's is a friend of mine."

"But don't you need it?"

"Not no more," said Psycho. "Turns out a Corolla that does three hundred MPH ain't exactly street legal. See what you can do with it, kid. Who knows? Maybe you'll break a speed record."

# 11

# IF AT FIRST YOU FAIL . . .

It was after midnight when Alex and Todd made it back to the Trumble house. They crept in the back door, then, quiet as thieves, went up to the turret. You know what it's like late at night, when everyone in the world is asleep? That's the kind of spooky it was when the friends went to work on the machine, which was where they left it, fixed to the posts.

Alex opened the iPod with the tiny screwdriver that Psycho had given him. The circuits inside were arranged as neatly as the houses of the subdivision. He connected the wires as he had been told, closed the back, and wound the whole thing—the hand wringer and the iPod—together with tape.

"Light the candle," said Todd.

Alex pressed some buttons on the iPod and then flashed the laser pointer at the first mirror. The light began to travel around the square, faster and faster. As it did, the hand wringer crackled and threw off sparks. The light was moving faster now, whipping around the square. Some papers on the desk fluttered, and the

floorboards creaked. Alex gathered his pennies and, one at a time, tossed them through the square. Though the light was moving and the hand wringer was humming and the room itself was glowing, the pennies acted as the one magical penny had acted before: shimmering as they moved through the square, but landing with a sad clank against the windows across the room.

This second failure was almost too much to take. Todd put his arm across Alex's shoulders and said, "We'll get there."

When Todd left, Alex got into his sleeping bag and watched the light move around the square. Scout snuggled beside him. He was out of ideas and felt just as useless as that red beam of light.

# 12

# WHERE THE DOG WENT

Alex sat up in the morning, rubbed his eyes, and looked across the room. The machine was still going, the beam blazing around the square. He held a sheet of paper in front of the mirrors. He was in the habit of turning off or shutting down whatever he was not using, even if there was no need. Alex went downstairs and poured himself a glass of juice. He got Scout's food out of the cabinet. Normally, Scout materialized as soon as she heard the cabinet door open, but this morning she was nowhere to be seen. Even when Alex poured the food, which was the equivalent of a bugle call for Scout, she didn't show up. He whistled, called—nothing. He walked through the house, looking. Nowhere.

Scout had a habit of wandering off for hours, even days. She'd been wearing her collar, which meant she couldn't get too far. She was probably in the yard, in the shade of the juniper. Alex decided he would find her when he got home from school.

Alex talked to Todd by the main entrance where the kids were gathered when he got to school. It was a field trip day. The entire school was going to the Field Museum in Chicago. Alex and Todd talked about the machine, then Alex told Todd about Scout. "Don't worry about it," Todd said. "You know Scout likes to roam."

By nine A.M., the kids were loaded onto six yellow buses heading to the city. As the buses pulled into the turnaround in front of the museum, they could see the banner that announced a splashy new exhibit:

**ANCIENT MAN AND HIS PETS**

How One Canine Invented Civilization

The kids were marched into the rotunda, where each class was divided into groups, these having to do with age and malleability. The troublemakers were herded and surrounded by hard-case teachers, but the science-curious were sent off with a single adult.

Alex and Todd were in a group led by a bottom-heavy teacher known to the kids as Big Butt Baschnagel. They followed that butt from room to room, exhibit to exhibit as, in the olden days and before GPS, sailors followed the polestar.

They walked through rooms filled with dinosaur bones, sea monsters, artifacts of prehistoric man. Finally, and by now the kids were worn out, they walked into the exhibit of ancient man and his pets. There were dioramas showing men in tiny clothes riding on the backs of sea turtles. There were dioramas showing men with spears carrying birds on their forearms. There was a drawing of a little man, basically nude, walking in a forest with a squirrel on a leash. Alex got quiet when they went into the last room, dedicated to the canine that made civilization possible.

He read the paragraphs that explained the animal.

Thoropulis, a mystery hound, seems to have been the model for every trained dog to follow. She appeared on the North American plain in what is now Illinois, twenty thousand years ago, where she was worshipped by nomadic hunter-gatherers.

Her arrival was inexplicable. According to some, she was part of a race of dogs trained by gods in the heavens. According to others, she came from another planet or world. Though alone when found, Thoropulis was well behaved and seemed to know all sorts of tricks. In one, called "summoning the monkey," she raised a paw as if to shake hands. Some say the custom of hand shaking, so prevalent in business circles today, began with Thoropulis.

In this room, you will see a few of the thousands of likenesses of Thoropulis that were painted and carved in her time and in the generations that followed. She is considered the first domesticated dog, the mother of all house pets. It was her ferocious loyalty and skill as a guard dog that allowed the ancients to give up their wandering and plant cornfields. Within a generation of her arrival, the first towns had been built in this part of the world. This is why she is called the enabler of civilization.

Though she was worshipped, she always

seemed to be looking for something or someone, as if she was a creature who could not find her way back home, a quality that made her truly otherworldly.

In later years, she is said to have vanished.

Alex read over this placard three times, then wandered through the hall, looking at the paintings and sculptures of Thoropulis. He saw a mosaic, a picture made of colored tile, of a dog with a white body and a gray face. She was howling and fierce. He saw a cave drawing of the same dog, running, barking at a mammoth. The sky behind her was glowering, and ancient

men raised spears and shouted. He saw another painting, in which Thoropulis was sitting in the glow of a campfire, chewing the femur bone of a stag. He saw a sculpture, which, according to a sign, had been used in a temple as an object of worship. It was mahogany, and the teeth were sharp and the eyes clear. It was covered with wax stains, residue from worshippers' candles. He saw other pictures, too: Thoropulis running, eating, drinking from a mountain stream. He could almost hear Thoropulis racing through the woods.

Alex grabbed Todd by the arm. "Isn't this weird?"

"Weird how?"

"This dog is Scout."

"Lots of dogs look like Scout."

"You're not getting it," said Alex. "This dog more than looks like Scout. This dog *is* Scout!"

"Okay," said Todd, laughing, "tell me how a dog that lived twenty thousand years ago is Scout."

"Because I left the machine on," Alex whispered. "Scout must've gone through. That's why I couldn't find her this morning. She was in the yard, only she was in the yard twenty thousand years ago."

"I thought the machine didn't work."

"I thought so, too, but we were wrong. Maybe,

because it was the first time we used the hand wringer, it took a long time to warm up. I went to sleep with the light spinning, then, in the middle of the night, Scout got up and went into the dingus."

"And came out here," said Todd, motioning to the walls.

"Poor girl," said Alex.

"Why?" said Todd. "They worshipped her. And look at the stag bone she's gnawing on!"

"But did you read the placard, about how she always seemed to be looking for someone or something?" Alex said. "She was looking for me!"

"Here's what I don't get," said Todd. "This dog, Thoropulis, I've heard of her before, so how can it be the same dog? I knew the name Thoropulis before you built the time machine."

"It's simple," said Alex. "As soon as she went through, she became part of history, so we've always known about her."

"She was in the past all along?"

"Yeah, she went back in time, so, though she was born after me, and I knew her when she was a puppy, she also lived thousands of years before we were alive."

"I still don't get it."

"Scout left yesterday," Alex explained, "but whatever she does from here on happened thousands of years ago—because that's where she is. If she kills an elk tonight, you might realize you know the story and feel like you've known it forever. It's like with the baseball card. You tear one, the tear appears in the other. The tear is like the story of Thoropulis that pops into your memory. I know it sounds crazy," said Alex. "Sometimes it hurts my head just to think about it."

"What do you do then?" asked Todd.

"I stop thinking about it."

# 13

# DO YOU REMEMBER THE FUTURE?

As the yellow buses arrived back at school, Todd nudged Alex and pointed. In the distance, cruising along the street that ran past the school, Alex saw the van. He recognized it by the tinted windows, the dirt and dents, the strange headlights.

"Oh, jeeez!" Alex said.

"No, this is good. Maybe your brother's in there. We should tell the teacher to call the police."

"Those jerks will never be caught by the police."

"Why not?" asked Todd.

"Because the van's a time machine. If they see the cops, they'll just go into another time."

# 25 GLENCOE SCHOOL

“How do you know it’s a time machine?”

“From the description Zeke gave the cops in Eagle River,” said Alex. “He said the headlights spun around until they made a pool of light, then the van drove through the pool. That’s exactly how our time machine’s supposed to work.”

The van parked beside the bus, and Davy got out. Alex pulled on his backpack, ready to run.

“What do you think they want?” Todd asked.

“Probably realized they got the wrong brother.”

“What’re you going to do?”

"Go home, get in the time machine, and go back to the day my brother was kidnapped," said Alex. "I can't beat them here, but maybe I can get a jump on them back there."

As the kids were getting up to leave the bus, Todd stood on his seat. "Wait a second everyone," he yelled. "Those men in the van, outside the bus, they're the ones who kidnapped Alex's brother."

This sent the teachers and assistant teachers into a frenzy. Ms. Baschnagel ran off the bus to call the police.

"Now, here's what we do," Todd continued, ignoring all the commotion. "First, I'm going to stall them."

"They'll grab you," said Alex.

"Don't worry. I'm the meal that can't be digested. The rest of you head out with Alex, crowd around him, don't let those ninnies catch sight of him. Walk around the side of the school. Then, Alex, when you get clear, run straight home."

And that's how it happened. Even though the teachers tried to stop the kids, the students pushed their way through the door. Todd, who was first out, walked up to Little Davy and started asking questions. He asked the time, he asked the score of the Cubs game, he asked Davy if he believed in God, he asked if Davy knew the weight of a truck. When the rest of the kids got out, Davy tried to push Todd away, but Todd kept stepping in front of him, asking, "Why do birds fly south in the winter?" "Why do you have bad dreams if you eat dinner too close to bedtime?"

By the time Davy got fed up and pushed Todd to the ground, the kids had made it around the building and Alex was gone. Davy turned to throttle Todd, but Todd, thinking this would happen, had crawled up behind Davy and tied his shoelaces together. Davy stumbled and fell, then swore at Todd. "Wait till we get our hands on your friend. We'll see who's laughing then."

# 14

# WHY LITTLE DAVY IS LIKE THIS

Because I'm the narrator of this story, because I'm telling it, because I already know what happens and how it will end, though I've decided not to tell everything, not yet, anyway, I want to give you a fuller picture of Carl and Little Davy. They're not the complete morons I've so far described. In fact, the story of Carl and Davy is, by itself, a great one. If I were a movie critic, I would call it a sad, hair-raising heartbreaker, complete with pratfalls and fat jokes.

Carl met Little Davy in school. Carl's father worked in a titanium mine. Davy's father was a veterinarian. Carl was a great athlete. Davy was smart. He was skinny then, too, and nice. He was also full of curiosity and would sit on his porch watching the moon drift across the sea. In many ways, Davy and Carl were a flip version of Alex and Todd, what the boys might have been in another universe.

Davy had, in fact, invented the time machine long before (or long after; it depends on your point of view) Alex did the same thing. And it was this machine that brought Little Davy to the attention of Ben Blizzard, the general who, two hundred years from now, will try to take over the world.

In pursuit of this dream of world domination, Ben Blizzard sought out Little Davy and his friend Carl. Blizzard first heard of the time machine via that verbal network that connects the biggest people in a country to the smallest: gossip. Davy told a friend about the machine, and he told another friend, who told his uncle, who told a third cousin, who was related, by marriage, to a secretary in the office of Ben Blizzard.

As soon as Blizzard got the news, he called his lieutenants into his office and said, "I must have that time machine!"

I know what you're thinking.

Okay, fine. Ben Blizzard wanted Davy to do his bidding, but Davy was a good kid, an intelligent kid, why would he do it? Or, more simply, how did that Davy become this Davy, with the white van and the fat fingers?

It happened this way: Ben Blizzard got Davy into his palace, with soldiers out front and flying saucers overhead, and pulled back a curtain. Through that curtain he showed Davy the entire world, all the

money and gadgets and vacations and equipment he could imagine, all the power, too. He told him, "Little Davy, it can all be yours. You just have to give me the time machine." In short, Davy—and Carl, too, who was led to the same window—had his head turned and his mind twisted.

Davy now wanted the world, which Ben Blizzard (understanding people) always kept just out of reach by promising but not delivering, even after Davy had turned over the blueprints for the time machine. Ben Blizzard always put Davy off, saying, "Davy, you will get what you want, when I get what I want."

"What's that?"

"Total control."

All this wanting without getting made Davy first eccentric, then diabolical. In this way, he became the most dangerous kind of character: the kid with just one thought in his head—give Ben Blizzard what he wants, so Ben Blizzard can give me what I want. In this way, Little Davy, who had been clever and nice, became stupid and mean. And Carl? Well, Carl went along for the ride. None of this should make you feel too sorry for Little Davy and Carl, by the way. As any cop will tell you, every killer has a story.

# 15

# TIPS FOR TIME TRAVELERS

While I've been telling you about Carl and Little Davy, Alex has made his getaway. He safely navigated the streets of town and ran into his house, the white van close behind. He shut the door, raced up to the turret, and dropped his backpack as he slid across the floor, pressing the laser pointer, turning on the dingus, which powered up in a flash.

Alex typed his desired destination into the iPod: year, day, hour, minute, second. But in his haste, he pointed the laser in the wrong direction, sending the beam clockwise around the square. Then he stepped into the dingus. It was his first trip across time. There was a tremendous noise—it sounded like the wind, or water falling on rocks, but faded as soon as he stepped back out. (There were additional phenomena, cool ones, but I'm going to save those for later.) He felt like a huge hand had carried him across the sky, turned him around, then put him down in a place that was entirely familiar but also entirely strange: the same room but at another place in time. He checked his arms, legs, hands. Everything was fine, where it should be. He breathed a sigh of relief and looked around. He'd meant to go two weeks back but was not sure where he'd landed. He held his hand in front of the mirrors, shutting off the machine.

As he crossed the room, Alex realized everything was different. The turret had been fixed up, tidied. There were couches now, a TV, all kinds of adult stuff, including a desk, where his father worked. It felt like a happy place, where people laughed and good work was done. There was a newspaper on the desk. Alex checked the date. He had not gone into the past but into the future—two years into the future! He knew he should turn the machine back on, set the stopwatch for the correct date, and get his brother, but curiosity got the better of him. He had to know what life would look like in two years, when he was twelve. Would he still be best friends with Todd, would his brother have returned, would his parents still be miserable? Besides, he figured, when he did go back, he would go back to whenever he wanted to go back to, whether he left now or three hours from now. To a boy with a time machine, there is no such thing as a wasted day.

He took the mirrors off the posts and dropped them, with the duct tape still attached, into his pocket, along with the iPod and laser pointer. With this machine, the danger was not only that some enemy would lock the door behind you, but that the door itself would be removed, stranding you in the wrong time.

Alex went downstairs to see what was happening in the future. He was careful to keep out of sight, walk near walls, stay in the shadows. Would anything scare his mother more than coming across her own son, two years younger, like a page torn out of the past? And how would Alex feel, spotting not some stranger but his own self, as in a memory? This is me later, and this is me now. Of course, if he did see his later self, that meant his later self would remember the meeting, as it had already happened when the later self was the younger self.

Ugh, too much.

Alex went out of the house and walked toward town. It was one of those perfect blue afternoons you get once a year. He was happy knowing he was cheating, that he would get to live this singular day twice, in the future (now) and again when this future became the present. At a bend in the road known as the bloody curve—there had been a terrible crash there so far back that all the details had been forgotten—he saw a sports car parked under a Bodhi tree. The white trunk of the tree twisted as it climbed, breaking into corkscrewing branches, covered with flowers and leaves that patterned the road with shadows.

The car was black, with monstrous fins and an open hood, beneath which you could see the engine. It took Alex a moment to recognize the owner of the car, smiling as she leaned against the driver's door, blond hair pulled back and sleeves pulled above the elbow.

"You really were a cute kid," she said. "I mean, yeah, you look good now that you're older, more like boyfriend material, but you were all right at that age, too."

"Frankie Johnston?" said Alex, amazed.

She was older, of course, but as beautiful as ever. And she had clearly moved up a level with her cars.

"What's that?" Alex asked, admiring her vehicle.

"A '67 Camaro with a 396 behind the grille. But who cares when you can travel by time machine?"

So bizarre! Frankie knew what Alex was up to, what he was doing, and where he'd come from. "But how'd you know I'd be here at this exact time, in this exact place?"

"Psycho told me, so you must've told Psycho."

"Psycho? The guy who's short a few teeth?"

"Yeah. You're good friends now. He was busy, so he sent me over with something for you."

She handed him a hand wringer, the device that gave the dingus a needed boost, making time travel possible. "He said to tell you to swap the other for this one. It's going to give you a smoother ride and make it harder for people to follow you through. He said you'd know what that means."

Frankie got in her car and started the engine.

"Where are you going?"

"I've got a race in Calumet City," she said. "Go to town. You'll be completely freaked by what you see."

Alex took the dingus out of his pocket, pulled off the old hand wringer, then attached the new device. He wound it together with the same tape, which was starting to lose some of its stickiness.

Everything is a clock, Alex told himself. The earth moving around the sun is a clock. The ravine collapsing into the lake is a clock. And this tape losing its stickiness is a clock, too.

Alex walked past the flower shop into town. There was a banner stretched across Park Avenue, lamppost to lamppost, waving in the breeze.

When Alex got close enough to read it, his knees went weak and he stumbled, so much so that a man in seersucker put his hand on the boy's shoulder and said, "Easy there, young fellah. There'll be plenty of time for falling when you're my age."

"It's the banner," said Alex. "It surprised me."

"Isn't it wonderful?" said the man in seersucker. "Dalton Trumble has made our town famous!"

After the man walked on, Alex read the banner again.

Here's what it said:

Maybe you're wondering something like: How is the future so good and happy when Alex has not yet fixed the present? Has not yet saved his brother, rescued his family? Well, maybe another, earlier Alex already fixed these things and created this future. Or maybe there are an infinite number of Alexes leaving and returning, solving these problems again and again. It's the paradox. Once you open the door of time, the future can change the present. Which means the future can become the past. Years later, when Alex sits back and recalls his days of time travel, he will recall his own childhood as well as a future that has yet to happen.

Dazed, Alex wandered into the bookstore. Everywhere he looked, there was a picture of his father, a few pounds heavier, a few hairs grayer, smiling like Alex had never seen his father smile. A table in the center of the store was piled high with Dalton Trumble books. When Alex got close, he could see that all these were, in fact, the same book, a blockbuster, the cause of the celebration and hoopla. Alex picked up a copy. The title was in red letters that looked blurred with speed: *Alex and the Amazing Time Machine.*

There was a picture of three boys on the cover. One looked like Alex. He was holding a laser pointer. One looked like Steven. He was being pushed by unseen forces toward a white van. One looked like Todd. He was running toward Steven as if he wanted to help, an aluminum baseball bat in hand.

There were other things on the cover, too. The turret, the library, the lake covered with ice, Mrs. Trumble and her client, a shadowy figure with a question mark where his face should be, Thoropulis, her gray head held high.

It made Alex queasy. Knowing it was there already, that the future had happened, that his future was someone else's past. It made him sad, too, especially the picture of Thoropulis. Until then, he hadn't really thought about what Scout's trip through time meant. Only what it meant in terms of the machine. That it *worked*! He now felt sadness for the other things, the big things—that if he failed in his mission, he would probably never see his dog or his brother again.

The owner of the bookstore asked Alex if he needed help.

"No," said Alex, who, for a moment, thought he might puke. But he didn't puke. That's the key to life, he told himself. Not puking when you want to puke, because you've got more important things to do.

Just now, the most important thing was to get a copy of his father's book out of the store. If he could get the book back to the machine, then back to his own time, where his father was stuck, maybe the book could help his father finish the story. Alex checked his pockets for money. Nothing, nada, zero, zilch. This was a lesson Alex would take from that first morning in the future: don't time travel broke. The store owner went behind the counter. He stood there, studying a copy of *Alex and the Amazing Time Machine*. He looked at the cover, then looked at Alex, then back again.

Alex considered going out and begging for the money, or asking the bookstore owner if he would entertain a trade: his shoes for a copy of the book? He finally decided the only way was the dark way. He had to steal it. He was opposed to theft in principle. It was wrong. But these were special circumstances. Alex was taking the book so that the book could be written. He was not stealing. He was creating. He would swipe a copy off the pile so his father could write the book, without which there could be no pile. Of course, none of this would make sense to the store owner, who was rooted in this time like a nail pounded into a board. So Alex watched and waited. His task was made harder by the attention he had drawn to himself.

A customer finally came in. He asked the owner if he could help him find a book by Ron Mallett.

"There in the back," said the owner, "in science."

"Can you show me?" the customer asked.

The owner hesitated, not wanting to let Alex out of his sight. But the man insisted, so he went. When the owner got back, Alex was gone and the pile of books was one book shorter.

It was close to one P.M. when Alex returned to the house, the book shoved under his T-shirt. As he crept in the side door, he saw a kid going out the front, a big kid, with straight brown hair and broad shoulders. This kid, who had a cool, easy way about him, was with a beautiful girl. Only when the kid turned onto the road to town, and Alex saw him in full profile, did he say to himself, "Oh my God, it's me."

# 16

# DOES IT FEEL LIKE YOU'VE BEEN HERE BEFORE?

Alex ran up the stairs of the turret. He quickly reassembled the time machine, pasting the mirrors on the posts, wiring in the iPod. He punched in his time of desired arrival. He would return at the moment he left. He took the pointer out of his pocket and shot a burst of light into the first mirror, being careful to get the vortex turning counterclockwise. In a moment, the space inside the mirrors turned hazy. He saw flashes, images of the room on the other side of time. He took a breath and stepped through. There was that noise again. Then he was back in the room as it had been before his father's success, rundown and drafty. The atmosphere had changed. What had been a cheery, buoyant house was again sunk in the gloom of a family in the midst of a tragedy.

Alex dashed downstairs and, in two steps, was in his father's office, with its dark computer and its pages of unfinished book. He put the stolen book on top of those pages. It would confuse his father at first, maybe scare him—what's this book, and who wrote it, and where does it come from?—but he was smart and would figure it out.

Okay, you may ask, why am I so certain Dalton Trumble, upon finding this strange book on his desk, would know what to do?

Because not only am I your narrator—I *am* Dalton Trumble. And Dalton Trumble is Rich Cohen. And

Rich Cohen did find the book. And he did know what to do. I copied it page for page, then sent those pages to my editor, Christy Ottaviano, at Henry Holt in New York. Indeed, she published the book. Which is how you have it to read and argue with and question.

Of course, all of this presents a paradox, which is a fancy word for a puzzle that cannot be solved. (In fact, if you think about a paradox too intensely for too long a time, you'll go crazy; some people believe that this is what happened to me.) Take this book as an example. If I wrote it by copying it, and if it existed in the future where Alex stole it only because I wrote it, where did it come from in the first place? And who is the true author? And who is writing these lines about its creation? Were they already in the book that Alex stole? And if so, does that mean the book had been stolen previously, before Alex stole it, by a still earlier Alex? Like I said, a paradox is a puzzle you can go crazy trying to solve.

So let's not try to solve it, and just move on.

As soon as Alex had put the book on his father's desk, he raced back upstairs and typed a new date into the iPod. He would go back forty-two days and sixteen hours, arriving thirty minutes before his family—his mother, father, Scout, brother, and himself—left on that fateful trip to Wisconsin.

He was careful to make sure the beam was moving counterclockwise around the square, then stepped into the dingus. This time he closely examined what was on either side of him as he traveled.

Here's what he saw:

Everything that happened in the last six weeks happening again, only backward, in a single spot, at a single moment. Even so, nothing was hurried. He saw the sun set and rise, set and rise, set and rise. He saw his mother walk backward down the stairs and drive backward down the street. He saw the town fill with shadows, then light, then shadows. He saw men walking backward, carrying lettuce and asparagus from the supermarket to the trucks that drove backward down the highways to the farms. He saw a baseball travel backward from deep centerfield to the bat of a hitter, then back to a pitcher's hand, then glove. He saw the Trumbles' car, the Jeep Wagoneer, moving the wrong way along route 40, from Wisconsin, where his brother had been kidnapped, back through the little towns to the special town that was their home.

Then he was through, on the other side, standing at the window in the room.

Though nothing was very different—what are six weeks?—everything was changed. He was back before the disaster.

He took apart the time machine, dropping the pieces into his pocket. (That was the great thing about Alex's invention—it could be taken apart and, as long as the tape was still sticky, could be reassembled on any threshold.) He knew he would need it with him. If he planned to disrupt the schemes of the bad men, he wanted a fast getaway.

Looking out the window, he saw his father at the trunk of the car, packing the sleeping bags and fishing rods. He saw himself, Alex Trumble, walking up the driveway, saying something to his father, then heading into the house. Where did I go from there? he asked himself. I think I came up here and goofed on the computer. I'd better hide and not give myself away to myself.

Though Alex would have liked to have had a long talk with himself, to ask questions like "what were you thinking?" and "why?" he went downstairs and out the back door instead. He hid in the garage until his father was done packing. Taking care not to be seen, he went to the car, popped the trunk, and made himself a bed among the sleeping bags.

He didn't want to ride in the trunk, but he knew it was safe. There were vents for air and a button that let you open it from inside. It was not all that uncomfortable, just boring. He had the iPod but would not turn it on. He needed to save the power for his trips through time. He could usually find a wall socket when he needed a charge, but who wanted to take a chance in the woods?

A car trunk is not the best place to spend an afternoon, but Alex could think of no better way to shadow his family while keeping out of sight. He knew he had to be well rested and ready when he arrived at Camp Cherokee. Alex had just one chance to get this right. Get it right, and few will ever believe it really happened. Get it wrong, and the world is damaged forever.

# 17

# CAMP AIN'T NO VACATION

The Trumbles piled into the car. Alex heard his brother talking, his parents talking, and his own voice. He heard Scout run across the yard and jump into the back seat. The engine started, and the car raced down the highway.

The family reached camp after sundown. Alex knew they had arrived when he heard the tires crunch on the gravel. Before unpacking, the Trumbles went into the main hall to say hello to friends. Alex remembered this and counted on it. As soon as he heard the door to the hall swing shut, he popped the trunk and climbed out.

He grabbed a sleeping bag and, as he did this, remembered that his father, while unpacking the first time, had complained (and would complain) that the family was short a sleeping bag. "Darn it. I bet it's just sitting in the garage with nothing to do."

This meant that Alex made this trip before, at least once, perhaps a number of times. Last go-round he'd been the Alex in the back seat. This go-round, he was the Alex in the trunk. Next go-round . . . ? Well, he hoped there wouldn't be a next go-round.

Alex went to the equipment shed for supplies: a flashlight, a fishing pole, a tin of worms, a frying pan, matches. He tied this all up in a bundle, threw the bundle over his shoulder, and started walking.

Following an old logger's trail, he was soon above camp. He walked for two miles, until he found a clearing in the trees. He could see a dark place where the lake was lapping at the shore and, looking the other way, the yellow lights of Cherokee, where his family was intact and unaware of how happy they were.

He settled his sleeping bag on a bed of pine needles and dug a pit. He went through the trees, gathering twigs for kindling. He built a fire in the pit and lay in the heat of the flames as he looked at the stars.

Some of those stars died a long time ago, he reminded himself. Their light reaches us centuries after they've burned out. Every time you look into space, you're looking at the past, at a world that no longer exists. Some people are scared alone in the woods, but Alex loved the sound of the wind high in the trees.

Still, Alex was troubled that night. He was, after all, not at home but in a time where he didn't belong. Think of the havoc this could cause! What might happen, for example, if Alex went back still further and met his own father before Alex was born? What if Alex asked his father to see a baseball game and his father said yes and it just so happened that that was the very day Alex's father met his mother? Only now, because he was with Alex, his father did not meet his mother, and Alex was never born. *Poof!* Alex vanishes. But if Alex vanished, he wouldn't be around to invite his father to a baseball game, so his parents would meet and Alex would be born. *Bling!* Alex reappears.

Just be careful, Alex told himself. Time travel is a serious business, the most extreme sport.

The next morning, Alex, feeling somewhat more optimistic, took the fishing pole and the worms and stood on a point that went out into the lake. The worm hit the water and, an instant later, the shadow of the worm appeared, dancing on rocks on the bottom. The line went tight, the hook flashed, and the shadow vanished, swallowed by the walleyed pike Alex was pulling from the water. He restarted the fire from embers, cleaned and cooked the fish, and had his breakfast as the sun rose above the pine trees across the lake.

## 18

# WHEN THEY MAKE YOU EAT WORMS

At 3:05 in the afternoon, Alex walked toward Old Counselors Road. He wanted to get there before his brother and the bad men. Surprise would be his weapon. But he must have miscalculated because, when he neared the spot, he saw Zeke Anderson running the other way in a panic. "I'm too late," Alex said, cursing himself, and as he was cursing himself, he started to run to the end of the road, where he knew the van would be idling.

In his determination to catch the van, he forgot to be quiet and broke out of the trees in a clatter of branches. He stumbled and fell on the road, right at the feet of his brother, who was being held in a viselike grip by Carl.

Where's Little Davy? Alex wondered, and, in a moment, found out.

Davy grabbed Alex from behind by the shirt and lifted him into the air. Alex saw the trees whirl overhead, then was slammed into the ground, where he lay, coughing and catching his breath.

All the while, Davy was talking to Carl, his voice thick and slow and filled with scorn. "Well, look what fell from the sky, the great disappearing one, the mastermind genius, time-chaser, do-gooder, backyard-fence-hopper, punk!"

"What are you doing here?" Steven asked Alex, confused.

"Saving you."

"Enough!" Carl shouted. "We want answers, and we want them now."

"Answers to what?" asked Steven.

Then, turning to Alex, Steven asked, "Do you know these guys?"

"Shut up," Carl said. "Now answer me."

"How can I answer you if I shut up?" Steven said.

Carl pulled back his hand, held it for a moment. Alex and Steven could see his yellow fingernails packed with dirt and blood, his broken knuckles, and the lizard ring on his middle finger, then he slapped Steven across the face. Steven yelped. Each finger left a mark on his cheek. The bruise turned purple where the lizard ring caught Steven below the eye.

"You jerk," Alex shouted.

"Listen to the whiner," said Little Davy, laughing.

"When I say shut up, SHUT UP!" Carl yelled.

"Why hit him," said Alex, "when you know it's me you want?"

"What's going on?" Steven demanded.

"We're going to get answers out of you," Carl hissed.

"Right here, Carl? On the road?" asked Davy. "What if someone sees?"

"Get them into the van," said Carl, who looked at the trees, his hands on his hips, trying to calm down.

With one hand, Davy dragged Alex to his feet, then, with the other, took hold of Steven and marched the brothers to the van. They fought, of course, kicked and screamed, sending up a plume of dust, but it was no use. Little Davy was surprisingly strong. Just like that, the brothers were seated on a dirty rug in the back of the van.

There were two desks set up there, the kind you find in a kindergarten class, with built-in chairs. The boys were told to sit. Davy went outside to talk to Carl. Alex looked around the van. The dashboard was covered with dials, switches, and indicators, but the indicators didn't show miles-per-hour or temperature or oil. They showed hour, second, year.

"What kind of van is this?" Steven whispered, confused.

"It's a time machine."

"What?"

"We're in a time machine," said Alex. "These guys have come from the future looking for me."

"Why?"

"I'm trying to figure that out."

"You've gone completely mental," said Steven.

"Maybe," said Alex, "but this is a time machine."

The door opened and Davy sat down next to the brothers. You don't notice just how big and ugly a person is until you're right next to him. Davy's hair was coarse like wire, his face was covered with carbuncles and pustules, and his hands were like hunks of raw meat.

Carl handed Davy a plate, which he put down in front of Alex. It was covered with worms. "We call it dirt dinner," said Davy. "We're going to ask you questions, and you're going to tell us the truth."

"And every time you lie," said Carl, "or refuse to tell us something we want to hear, you're going to have another bite of dirt dinner."

Alex got that awful feeling where a little puke comes up into your mouth and you have to swallow hard to keep it down.

"All right, Alex, how 'bout you tell us where we can find the dingus?" asked Davy.

"How do you know his name?" Steven asked.

"From the history books," said Davy. "Now just shut up."

"Yeah," Carl said to Steven, "or I'll order you dinner from the same restaurant."

"And when he says dinner," said Davy, "he means worms!"

Little Davy asked Alex dozens of questions. Whenever he got an answer he didn't like, he wound the fork in worms, gathering them up like spaghetti, then held the fork to Alex's lips. At first, Alex kept his teeth clinched, but Davy made Alex open. Davy did this in a way I won't share, as I don't want to scare the squeamish, but it's enough to say that Alex ate the entire plate, could feel the worms wriggling on his tongue and going down his throat, and that he never would like them, even if he had ketchup.

After thirty minutes of this food torture, Alex was grossed out and angry. "Just what is it you want?" he demanded.

"We want you to stop thwarting our plans," said Carl.

"How have I thwarted your plans?"

"We were a whisker from getting everything we wanted, all those things that were shown to us in the window, when you retrieved that man now called Dimwitty from the past, where we stashed him," said Carl. "We could've killed him, of course, but we're not killers, and we're paying for that weakness now."

"What did you do with him?" Alex asked.

"You know what we did," said Davy. "He's your mother's client. We sent him to the past and got him jailed so he could do no harm, but you sent him back with your dingus, and he overthrew Ben Blizzard, and without Ben Blizzard, we're nothing."

"And now," said Davy, close to tears, "Dimwitty is a hero, and we're villains, and you fill the history books."

"Who's Dimwitty?" asked Steven, totally confused.

"Mom's client," said Alex.

"If she'd kept her nose out of it, none of this would be happening," said Carl.

"Do you mean the guy with no memory," Steven asked, "and the wallet filled with odd bills, dollars with strange faces on the front and the weird device on the back?"

"Ha!" said Davy. "Strange faces on the front . . . weird device on the back. . . . Those strange faces are the faces of our emperors, you idiot!"

"Then how come we've never heard of them?"

"Because you live now," said Carl, "and those men are leaders in the future, two hundred years from now."

"What's the device on the back?" Alex asked.

"The dingus," Carl growled.

"What's the dingus?" Steven asked.

"Your brother's time machine," said Little Davy.

"Why are you so bent out of shape by a time machine when you already have a great time machine of your own?" asked Alex.

"Good question!" said Davy.

"And thank you for your kind words about my time machine," said Carl.

"*Our* time machine!" said Davy.

"I'll tell you why we're after it, but only once, so

listen. Carl and I were all set to make it big—as soon as Ben Blizzard became emperor, we'd get our reward."

"We'd have power then," said Carl. "And we'd finally tell all the snobby high-hats we went to school with to stick it! All we had to do was get rid of Dimwitty, who wanted to dispose of Ben Blizzard and return control to the people."

"The nobodies," said Davy.

"So we conked Dimwitty on the coconut, conked him good, too, so he wouldn't remember nothing," said Davy with a laugh, "then brought him back here and dumped him at the scene of a crime."

"When the police found him, they thought he'd done the crime and put him in jail, and there could be no alibi, 'cause he came from the future," said Carl.

"But there were dead bodies at the scene of that crime," said Alex.

"Well, we wanted him locked up for life, and, in this time, that means murder," said Davy.

"But where did the dead bodies come from?" asked Alex.

"Where do you think?" said Carl with a laugh. "We found two living thugs and turned them into dead people."

"That makes you murderers," said Alex.

"It's not murder," said Carl. "It's politics."

Okay. Maybe I need to stop here and explain the big picture, which is chaos on the ground and might have confused you, but is clear from a distance. It's the great thing about being the writer of a story. You can see what it's like in the heat of the moment, where the bad men cruise by in the van, but you can also see what it's like from above, where everything is obvious.

Far in the future, two hundred years from now, an evil dictator named Ben Blizzard takes over the world, making the many nations of the earth into a single super nation. In the end, a freedom fighter, known here as Dimwitty, is the only person who stands between Blizzard and total control.

Carl and Davy are ordered to "dispose of the problem," which is why Dimwitty is sent to the past and framed. But as smart as Carl and Davy might be—Davy did build the time machine, after all—Alex proves just a little bit smarter, building the dingus and returning Dimwitty to his own age, where Dimwitty overthrows Ben Blizzard. Rather than admit failure, Carl and Davy are now trying again, going back still further in time to confiscate the dingus before it can be used, or else stop Alex Trumble altogether.

"You're coming after us because our mom took that case?" Steven asked.

"No," said Davy. "We're coming after you because your brother built the dingus."

"Last chance," said Carl. "Where is the dingus?"

Alex suddenly realized that he did have what they wanted: the dingus was in his back pocket.

Did he tell Carl and Davy this?

Of course not.

"Sorry," he said. "I never built any such device and wouldn't know how to build it even if I wanted to."

The men looked at each other, considering.

"What do you think?" Davy asked Carl. "Is it possible? Did we travel back too far, have we arrived too early?"

Davy and Carl whispered together as Alex thought nervously about time. Zeke must have arrived back in camp by now, told Mr. and Mrs. Trumble about the van and the kidnapping, gathered the group of people, and headed back down Old Counselors Road. Alex knew he was in that crowd himself. If Carl and Davy saw another Alex, they'd know he had lied about the dingus. If he was here and there, he had obviously mastered time. Alex was in no mood to see how these men would react to that information.

"Okay, Davy figured it out," Carl told Alex. "Our real problem is not the dingus, it's you."

"That's right," said Davy, "and we've tried to stop you by getting the machine, but if we can't get the machine, we have to stop you from time traveling the old-fashioned way."

"We have to take you out of time altogether."

The brothers fell silent. The blood drained from their faces, and they looked at each other.

"You should have stuck with baseball," said Steven.

"Yeah, I know," said Alex.

"Out of the van," Carl ordered.

"One thing first," said Steven.

"What's that?" asked Carl.

"I think your van looks like a piece of garbage."

"Oh, come on," said Davy, "you don't really believe that."

"Of course he doesn't," said Carl. "He's only being mean because he knows we're about to kick him out of time."

They were led into the trees. Davy tied their hands behind them, then tied their feet so they couldn't run. Carl went back to the van and returned with a rectangular case, the sort you might use to carry a flute or oboe.

Carl set the case on the ground and opened it with a snap of buckles. He took out a kind of gun Alex had never seen. Unlike most guns, where the barrel is straight as a ruler, this weapon, which the bad men called "the gizmo," had a corkscrew barrel, twisty as a roller coaster. The bullet, which was a pulse of light, went around and around before exiting the gun with a flash and entering the body of the poor jerk who'd just been shot.

"What is it?" asked Alex.

He was scared, yes, but even in this moment of terror, he didn't lose his curiosity. The scientific part of him, the machine-maker soul, stayed at a remove, ten to twenty feet above the action, watching and taking notes.

"It's an Entreasure Six," said

Davy, running his hand along the stock—shoulder rest, telescopic sight, and trigger.

"Only three were ever made," Carl said. "Only two ever worked."

"And we've got one of those," said Davy.

"What does it do?" Alex asked.

"Interesting question," said Davy, "and normally, since you're about to find out, and since there is nothing for knowing like personal experience, I would not take the time to tell you. But as I see in you a kindred spirit, another person driven by a need to know, I will tell you."

"If you're going to tell him, tell him already," said Carl, getting impatient.

"It works like this," said Davy. "Every time you reach a crossroads in life and hesitate while you make up your mind—Should I take the snowboard or the skis? Should I have the hot dog or the burger?—you really make both choices."

"This sounds familiar," said Alex. "Is this the parallel universe theory?"

"Nothing theoretical about it," said Davy. "Say, for example, you chose a hamburger over a hot dog. It seems you're one boy eating a hot dog. But the universe has, in fact, forked. Where there was one, there are now two. In the first you eat a hot dog; in the second you eat a hamburger."

"Enough," said Carl, yanking the gun from Davy's hand. "It throws you out of this universe and into one of the zillions of parallel universes where you do not build a time machine, meddle in future politics, and become a giant pain in my butt. That's all you need to know."

Carl raised the gun. Alex could feel the barrel pressing into his back. It was steely, and the direness of the situation occurred to Alex. He was about to be blasted from his familiar world into a twin world from which there would be no escape.

He suddenly remembered how, when he was a kid, he stood in his parents' room, looking in his mother's full-length mirror, dreaming of stepping through the glass into that other world where everything would be the same and not the same, backward, unearthly, unsettling, odd. And that's where he stood again, on the threshold, about to cross to the other side.

Carl threw a switch, and the gun hummed to life.

Alex closed his eyes. In that moment, he noticed everything: the cry of a falcon, the breeze on his face, the sound of a distant stream. Further still, he heard voices and footsteps and knew this was the crowd from camp, his parents, his dog, himself, coming up the road, arriving too late.

Too late, he knew, because he had lived this moment before, as part of the crowd, and he knew his parents never did see the van. They would see nothing but open road and weeds.

Have you ever thought about the nature of time? It's funny. It seems like some things are just supposed to play out in a certain way. If you try to change them, you end up making them happen. The bad men, trying to stop Alex from building the dingus, kidnapped his brother, causing Alex to create the very device they feared. Alex, trying to prevent a tragedy, went after his brother, which, it seemed, was only going to compound the tragedy, adding his own disappearance to that of Steven.

Alex turned to get a last look at his world. As he did, he saw a patch of air behind Carl and Davy turn hazy. Then, out of the patch, Todd Johnston came at a run, an Easton aluminum baseball bat in hand. He swung as hard as he could, catching Carl below the knee, sending him to the forest floor, where he lay grimacing.

The gun went off as Carl fell. Alex could hear the light bullet cutting through the leaves at the top of the canopy. It left a tunnel of space, missing foliage sent to some parallel universe. Without breaking stride, Todd turned and swung again, hitting Little Davy dead solid on the knee. He, too, went down, moaning.

Todd took the gun from Carl's hands. While covering the bad men, he untied Alex and Steven. "Take the rope and tie up those fools."

"How'd you know?" Alex asked.

"What did you think I was going to do when you disappeared?" asked Todd. "A person doesn't get many best friends."

"But what about the machine?" asked Alex. "I've got it in my pocket, so where did this one come from?"

"I went to the turret after you vanished, and there it was," said Todd. "It's like with the baseball card. The same machine from a different place in time."

Alex heard people on the road, voices, his own among them. "Hurry," he said, "here they come."

"Here who comes?" asked Todd.

“Me and my family,” said Alex.

“Okay, on your feet,” Alex instructed Davy and Carl.

Alex told Todd to march the men into the woods. “I’ll be right there.”

He walked over to the van, opened the driver’s door, started the engine, and pressed a bunch of buttons. The headlights came on and began to spin. Alex put the car in drive and jumped away. The van rolled up the road, then disappeared through its own window of fuzzy light.

When Alex caught up with the others, Davy was crying, tears streaming down his great fat face.

“You mean, mean boy,” said Carl. “Where did you send our baby?”

“To the end of time,” said Alex.

Alex could see the crowd through the trees. He could see his parents, the police, Scout, himself. His parents looked terrified. He wanted to haul his brother out of the woods and stand him at their feet. But he had to fight the impulse.

“What do we do with them?” Todd asked, looking at Carl and Davy.

“I sent the van to the end of time,” Alex said. “Let’s send them to the beginning.”

"How do you feel about snuggling with a T. rex?" Steven said, poking Little Davy in the ribs.

Little Davy moaned.

Alex took the mirrors from his pocket and began fixing them to the trunks of the trees. Twin pines, their trunks as straight as arrows, standing two feet apart. He stuck the mirrors on with the duct tape, still coiled into loops, as sticky as ever. He then wired up the iPod and typed in the destination: 300,000 B.C. Little Davy was sobbing. Carl scowled and called him "a big baby."

"What stops them from using the machine to come back or go after the van?" asked Todd.

"If I reverse the laser as soon as they're in, the door should close behind them."

Todd nodded.

Alex flashed the pointer and the laser began to turn around the square. The space inside went hazy, and the world on the other side appeared in the mist, desolate, cold, and white.

"All right," said Todd, pointing the gun. "Get in there."

Carl and Davy stood at the threshold, hands raised, backs to the old world.

"Don't do it," said Carl. "We'll never survive. It's murder."

"It's not murder," said Alex. "It's politics."

"I'd rather you shoot us with the gun," said Carl. "That would be better."

"Okay, if that's what you want," said Todd, raising the weapon.

"No, no," screamed Davy, and both men tumbled backward into the dingus. Alex cleared the square, then quickly got the light going in the opposite direction, sealing the door behind Carl and Davy.

The crowd had gone back to camp. The boys stood for a moment, stunned, breathing in the smell of pine needles.

"What now?" Todd asked.

"We each go to our own time and keep our mouths shut so we can meet again in the future."

Alex explained in detail. Todd would take his machine back to his point of departure. Alex would do the same. Steven would walk back to camp, where his parents would greet him with relieved hugs and tears.

"What do I tell them?" Steven asked.

"Make something up," said Alex. "Tell them you

got lost, went for ice cream, fell in a hole, got trapped by a bear, were abducted by aliens, anything."

Before he went, Steven said, "Hey, Alex, I take back all the bad stuff I ever thought about you."

"You were thinking bad stuff about me?" asked Alex, laughing.

"You know what I mean. I just didn't understand."

"I always loved you enough for both of us," Alex said.

"Now that we're all in love," Todd said, "don't you think we should get back home before the iPod runs out of juice?"

A moment later, Todd was through the tunnel and back in his own time. (He hung on to Little Davy's gun, which he stashed in his closet with his batting gloves and hockey sticks.) Alex soon had the laser spinning around his own square. Before stepping into the dingus, he took the baseball card out of his pocket and dropped it into a raspberry bush.

19

# THE QUICKEST WAY OUT OF JAIL

Alex stepped out of the dingus into the woods nearly six weeks later—two days shy of his old present to be exact. He wanted to leave himself time to get home and take care of a piece of business on the way. Walking along the main road, he caught a ride to town on the back of a slow-moving watermelon truck. The day was sunny and fine. Having learned his lesson on that first trip, he had grabbed enough money in his house for a bus ticket to Illinois. He slept the entire way, the side of his forehead leaving a small perspiration stain on the dirty Greyhound glass.

He did not go straight home but stopped at the Cook County jail instead. It was visiting day. He asked the woman at the front office if he could see prisoner Dimwitty.

Alex was led to a room where inmates sat with their families: crying wives, bewildered children. A forlorn scene. Dimwitty was brought out. Tall and handsome, his hair was steel gray. Having recovered much of his memory, he was not surprised to see Alex. He had, in fact, been expecting him. He remembered Alex from the future and knew from the history books just what Alex would do next: how he would call over the guards, distract them with a nonsense story about a stolen wallet and a missing lady, then use the ensuing confusion to fix the mirrors of the dingus to the legs of the table he was sitting at and get the laser beam going.

Alex punched a number into the iPod when no one was looking: 200 years in the future. All Dimwitty had to do was pretend he dropped something, get on his hands and knees, and crawl through the wormhole. *Poof!* Gone.

Alex dropped the pieces of the device in his pocket, jumped up, and screamed, "Oh my God! He vanished!"

When the perplexed warden questioned him, Alex said, "You know, this is just the sort of strange thing that happens in Glencoe. I suspect aliens."

The warden knew Alex's mother. He called Mrs. Trumble and told her to come get her son.

On the way home, Mrs. Trumble asked Alex a thousand questions. She asked why he was at the jail, how he had gotten there, why he had gone to the city. He felt like he was a witness in one of her trials, and, like a witness in one of her trials, he spoke a lot but said nothing. She finally gave up, sighed, and, changing the subject, said, "Well, we finally got some good news today."

"What's that?" asked Alex.

"Your father's book has been reviewed in the *Tribune*. There's a copy in back."

Alex was surprised. How had the book been published so soon? All his traveling had apparently altered the time-space continuum in a mysterious way. He picked up the newspaper and turned to the arts page. There was a picture of the book's cover just as Alex had seen it in the future—the boys, the turret, and Scout. This book was, according to the reviewer, a meditation on time and destiny.

"How does Dad come up with this stuff?" Alex asked, smiling.

"Easy," said Mrs. Trumble. "He remembers the future, and he imagines the past."

# THE FROZEN CHOSEN, OR AN ATTEMPT AT A POSTSCRIPT

A month later, on the first day of summer, with the trees billowing like sails, Alex was involved in an extra-inning softball game, which ended when he drove the twelve-inch into the shed on the lonely side of left field. The runners circled the bases, and Alex touched them all, ending at home in a shower of high fives. One of his friends called it a God ball "because it went so high it touched heaven."

Alex got a ride home from Frankie Johnston, who had been driving past the field. It was fun to drive with Frankie, to ride shotgun in one of her powerful machines, in this case a '64 Chevelle.

Frankie asked Alex if he'd seen Todd, who hadn't come home after school. "No," said Alex, "but I'll keep an eye out."

Alex ran up to the turret as soon as he got home. Something wasn't right. He could feel it. He looked around, wondering, examining, when suddenly the air in the corner grew hazy and Alex could see white cliffs and snow, then Todd stepped out of the square. He was wearing an animal skin and carrying a spear in his right hand; a dog with a white body and a gray face was under his arm. Alex shared a confused glance with the dog, then shouted, "Scout!"

Scout jumped out of Todd's arms and bounded across the room, wiggling like a fish, tail flicking back and forth.

"How long were you there?" Alex asked Todd.

"Long enough to master the art of spearfishing and saber-toothed tiger baiting. You can't believe how hard it is to dognap an animal from a tribe convinced that the dog is a god."

* * *

Alex wrote Dr. Shaprut as soon as he had a chance. He told her everything. She was now planning a trip to Illinois, where she would talk to Alex and see the dingus for herself. She wanted to discuss the dangers of time travel. Alex knew she was thinking of her own family, crushed all those years ago in the elephant stampede at the circus.

The following year, Alex's school took another trip to the Field Museum. This time, the featured exhibit was called *The Struggle of Early Man.* It featured two nomads who'd been found frozen in a crevasse in northern Minnesota. It took the boys about a minute to realize who they were looking at—Carl and Little Davy, in skins, harried and miserable on the other side of time. Special attention was paid by curators to a lizard ring on the tall one's middle finger. It was said to mark him as a member of an ice cult, the follower of a strange faith. On the way out, the boys went into the gift shop, where Alex was proud to see a display of his father's book *Alex and the Amazing Time Machine.*

The friends sat on the steps of the museum, the city stretching away before them. They talked about

THE STRUGGLE OF EARLY MAN

the book and how strange it was that Alex had brought it back from the future so it could be written in the past.

At the very least, thought Alex, it shows how serious this business of time travel really is. A lot of terrible things could happen, that was clear. Once you started messing with the chain of events, the series of happenings that underpin our lives, there was no telling where it would end.

"I feel bad about Carl and Davy," Alex said. "I wanted to get rid of 'em, but their fate seems a little too cruel."

"Don't worry," said Todd, smiling. "We've still got the dingus. We can always go back and save them."

I have spent a good deal of time thinking about how to end this book. Should I leave it here, on the steps of the Field Museum, where Alex and Todd dream of future travels into the past? Or should I take a step back, pull away, as a movie camera does when the director wants to show you not just the house but the town, not just the town but the country, not just the country but the planet, a blue marble in the immensity of space? So here it is, your parting shot, the picture you stare at while the credits roll: me, the narrator, Dalton Trumble (or Rich Cohen, if you prefer) in my office in the turret, the lake lapping at the shore below, already at work on another, even more astounding adventure. Did I ever tell you about the time Alex stumbled across a lost island?